Phillip stared at his friend in complete and utter disbelief.

The last time he'd had a serious girlfriend, they spent every moment together until the relationship cooled and she dumped him. Since Neil had been going out with Grace for about a year, the excitement of a new relationship was apparently over. Still, Phillip figured that if he had a steady girlfriend, he would much rather spend the time with her than watching a hockey game, regardless of who was playing, at least until the play-offs.

"Come on, Neil. Let's go."

"I said go without me. Grace won't mind. She's probably just going to tell you all about how she fixed your angel. You don't need me for that."

Phillip opened his mouth, about to tell Neil that if that were the case, then he could watch the game just as well from Grace's couch as from their own, but he stopped short. Since Neil and Grace had started going together, Phillip hadn't been able to understand their relationship. Therefore, he wasn't likely to figure it out today.

"Fine," he snapped, not at all trying to keep the edge of sarcasm out of his voice. "Is there a message or anything you want me to pass on?"

"Naw. See you later." Without waiting for a response, Neil turned up the volume on the television.

GAIL SATTLER

lives in Vancouver, British Columbia (where you don't have to shovel rain) with her husband, three sons, two dogs, five lizards and countless fish, many of whom have names. She writes inspirational romance because she loves happily-ever-afters and believes God has a place in that happy ending. Visit Gail's website at www.gailsattler.com.

GAIL SATTLER

His Christmas Angel

HEARTSONG
PRESENTS

Dedicated to Sandie, for whom crocheting will never be the same. Thanks for everything.

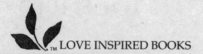

™ LOVE INSPIRED BOOKS

Recycling programs for this product may not exist in your area.

ISBN-13: 978-0-373-48758-5

HIS CHRISTMAS ANGEL

Heartsong Presents/November 2013

First published by Barbour Publishing.

Copyright © 2002 by Gail Sattler

Cover illustration by Lorraine Bush.

www.Harlequin.com

Printed in U.S.A.

Chapter 1

"You're finally home. What's in the bag?"

Phillip McLean kicked the door closed behind him, sauntered into the middle of the living room, and laid the big blue plastic bag on the coffee table. "Believe it or not, it's a Christmas decoration."

Phillip's best friend and roommate, Neil, shook his head, then quirked one eyebrow as he stared at the bag. "But it's not even Thanksgiving. Why did you buy a Christmas decoration?"

Very slowly, Phillip reached inside the bag. "I didn't buy it, and it's not just any decoration. It's Granny's angel. The one that goes on top of the Christmas tree." As gently as he could, Phillip lifted out his family's treasured heirloom to show his friend. "She made it herself. Isn't it great?"

Phillip didn't know how something made entirely out of threads not even as thick as two-hundred-pound test monofilament fishing line maintained its solid posture, yet it did. As a child, the angel's construction had fascinated him, and it still did, even as an adult.

From the top of its head to the bottom of the flowing gown, the brilliant white angel stood about ten inches tall. Its intricately patterned wings extended to the sides with a wingspan of what Phillip figured had to be nearly a foot. The flowing gown was made in the same way, with a variation of complex bumps and patterns. Some kind of shiny fabric lined the gown, which added a distinct richness to it, as well as prevented any green from being seen inside the angel once it gained its place of honor atop the Christmas tree.

The pale golden yellow hair was so soft and curly that Phillip always wondered if it was real, even though he knew it couldn't be, which added to the fascination. Atop the angel's head, a circle of gold beads strung on a piece of stiff wire formed a halo.

In stark contrast to the crisp white of the angel itself, the bright, cherry-red embroidered rosebud mouth and antique china eyes gave the angel a fragile and almost surreal beauty.

All his life, every Christmas of his twenty-seven years, except for opening gifts as a child, Phillip's favorite part of Christmas Day was when Granny's beautiful angel made its appearance. And now, the angel was his.

Grinning widely, Phillip held it out toward Neil.

Neil didn't take it. Instead, Neil squinted one eye and folded his arms over his chest. "If it's your granny's, what are you doing with it?"

"Remember, in a couple of weeks Granny is moving into the senior citizens' complex. She's getting rid of most of her stuff because she's going from a fully furnished three-bedroom house into a one-bedroom apartment."

Neil glanced around the room, then back to the delicate angel. "If she's getting rid of her stuff, then why didn't you take her spare couch, instead? You know. That big comfy one she has in the basement."

Since Neil didn't want to examine the angel, Phillip tucked the plastic bag he'd brought the angel home in under his arm, pushed aside Neil's coffee mug and the stack of magazines, then gently set the angel onto the center of the coffee table. "I'm getting the couch on the weekend. A bunch of my cousins are meeting at Granny's, and she's going to divide up all her extra furniture and stuff then. But I got to take the angel home today." He still could hardly believe the treasured angel had found a new home, even if it was temporarily in the middle of his messy coffee table.

"I guess," Neil mumbled. "If you're into that kind of thing."

Unable to wipe the smile off his face, Phillip lowered himself to sit beside Neil on the couch. "You don't understand. Granny made this angel when she first got married to my grampa. She started what we do every Christmas morning when my aunt Helen was born. Granny would put a nativity set on the floor beside the Christmas tree for the whole Christmas season. On Christmas morning, when everyone arrived, Mary and Joseph would make a trek across the living room, and baby Jesus would be born in the manger in the wooden stable. Then, Grampa would lift up whoever's turn it was to put the angel on top of the tree. Once the angel was in place, the shepherds and sheep would go to see the baby Jesus, and so would the three Wise Men and their camels. It was a real production. Playing out the Christmas story with actual figures and a *'real'* angel really brought the message home. The birth of Jesus and the events of the day really came alive for us when done with figures we could see and touch. When my grampa finished telling the story, we'd pray and then open the gifts. The whole time, it was almost like the angel was watching over us and smiling. It always made Christmas Day even more special."

Neil smirked. "That sounds like an interesting thing to do every Christmas. When I was a kid, we just tore into the gifts like little savages."

"Not us. My family is civilized." Phillip waited for Neil to respond accordingly, but Neil merely grunted.

Phillip leaned forward and gently ran his fingers over the tip of one of the angel's wings. "Now that us grandkids are all grown, even though none of us have kids of our own yet, we still take turns putting up the angel. Just now we're all tall enough not to need a boost. But my cousin Trevor and his wife, Janice, are going to have a baby soon, so next Christmas we'll have a new member of the family to share our tradition with. Granny's really excited about that."

"If it's a big family tradition, then why did she give you the angel? And what about the rest of the set?"

"The rest of the set is different. They're made for kids to play with. As they get wrecked or tattered, she throws them out and makes another new one out of whatever she's got handy. So she just packs them all up in a box with the rest of the Christmas decorations. But the angel is special, so no one ever plays with it. Besides, it goes on top of the tree and stays there, I guess because it's made differently. She always said that one day she would give it to one of the grandkids, and I got first dibs. Granny is terrified that it might get lost or damaged when she's moving or accidentally sold in her garage sale by a well-meaning friend. She's getting rid of so much stuff, she can't keep track of everything. That's why I got the angel now."

Hesitantly, Neil picked up the angel to examine it. "If she made it when she first got married, this thing's gotta be really old." Neil poked at one of the wings, then wiggled it to test its solidity. "What are you going to do with it?"

Phillip rested his elbows on his knees as he watched Neil fiddle with his new prized possession. "I figure I'll keep it out for awhile, you know, display it for a few days. Then I'll just put it back in the bag and keep it in the closet. We don't have a nativity set or kids to play with it, so I'll just put the angel on our own tree when we set it up. Since my family is doing Christmas at my parents' place this year, I'll take it with me on Christmas morning. That way we can still do the usual Christmas thing with it."

Neil wiggled the other wing, then very carefully returned the angel to its place on the coffee table. "I don't know how long ago your granny got married, but your mom is over fifty, and your aunt is even older than that. This angel's got to have some kind of heirloom status by now. Old stuff is usually treated real special. I don't think this thing should just be stuffed in a bag and mashed into the back of the closet."

Phillip's smile dropped, and he stiffened to lean all the way back into the couch. "I never thought of that. You're probably right. Maybe I should phone my mom. She'll know what I should do with it until the Christmas season."

As Phillip shuffled to the end of the couch and reached for the phone, Neil returned his attention to the television. He picked up the remote control from beside him on the couch at the same time as he groped in the air for his coffee mug with his free hand.

"Neil!" Phillip mumbled as he paused from dialing his parents' phone number. "Watch it. You're going to—"

Because the mug wasn't where Neil had left it, Neil misjudged its location and bumped the mug without actually gripping it. Almost in slow motion, coffee sloshed over the sides of the mug. The mug wobbled and then began to tip.

Phillip dropped the phone and lunged forward, but before he could grab the angel, the mug toppled. Coffee splashed into the air and onto the angel at the same time as a river of coffee spewed over the surface of the table. As the mug landed on its side, more coffee splashed out of the mug. In addition to the trail of brown spots that had splattered up the angel's side, more coffee seeped into the bottom of the angel's gown.

Phillip scooped up the angel at the exact second the stream of coffee reached the edge of the table and ran over onto the carpet. The dampness of the coffee in the formerly white gown warmed his hand at the same time as more coffee, cooler from its journey down the coffee table, dripped down onto his foot. Large splotches of brown marred the angel's gown, and one complete side of the angel was dotted with brown coffee freckles.

He stood in silence, barely able to believe what had just happened if it weren't for the evidence in his hand.

"Phil! I'm sorry! It was an accident."

All Phillip could do was stare at the angel in his hands.

"I'll get it cleaned! I promise!"

Phillip blinked a few times, then raised his head and met Neil's eyes. "How? Coffee stains. I still have a brown spot on my favorite white T-shirt that I couldn't get out from like six months ago. Granny's going to kill me."

Neil ran one hand over his face. "What time is it? Maybe we can take it to the dry cleaners."

Phillip checked his watch. "Everything is closed by now. Maybe we can phone someone who can help us."

Neil ran for the church directory and frantically began paging through it. "I bet Mrs. Carruthers would know what to do."

Phillip shook his head. "Forget it. She's Granny's best friend. I need to keep this a secret."

"What about Mrs. Kenaston? She'd know."

Phillip shook his head. "No. She knows Granny too well."

"Uh, Phil… Everybody knows your granny. There's no

way she won't find out what happened. I'm really sorry. I'll tell her it was all my fault."

Phillip sucked in a deep breath, then let it out in a rush of air. "I give up. Maybe I should just phone Granny and tell her before she hears it from someone else. She probably won't be mad, but she will be very disappointed in me. I guess the most important thing is that I can't take the chance the angel will be wrecked. Give me the phone."

Neil walked to the phone on the floor, which was now emitting a loud, annoying beeping from being off the hook for so long. Neil hung it up to stop the noise, but instead of picking it back up again to dial, he continued to press it down into the cradle. "Wait. I'm going to call Grace."

"Grace? Give me the phone, Neil. This isn't the time for you to be phoning your girlfriend. I need to call Granny before it's too late."

"No. You don't understand. Grace is really into that craft stuff. Remember? All year long she makes all sorts of things, then donates everything to the church bazaar. Lots of times when we go over to someone's house just to sit and talk, she brings knitting or stuff. I've seen her make some really pretty things out of the same stuff that angel is made of. I'll bet she would know what to do."

"What if she's in bed? It's getting late."

"Naw. Even if she is, she'll be glad to help."

Before Phillip could think to agree or disagree, Neil started dialing.

Grace Kramer stared at the clock as she listened to the voice on the other end of the phone. "Neil? Why are you calling at this hour?"

Her heart pounded while she waited for him to speak, fearing what he would say. No one ever called her past ten at night unless it was an emergency, least of all Neil. Over the past year since she'd been dating Neil, he seldom called after suppertime unless they had plans.

Neil cleared his throat. "You know Phil, my roommate?"

Grace's stomach knotted. "What happened to Phil?" She didn't know Phil very well, but as Neil's best friend, she was at least a little fond of him. She certainly didn't want anything bad to happen to him.

"Well, nothing happened directly, but I think I might have wrecked something of his. I was wondering if maybe you might know what to do before the damage becomes permanent."

Her heartbeat slowed while his unusual request began to sink in. "I'm really not good at fixing things. Maybe he should take it to the store he got it from in the morning, and they could tell him what to do."

"No. You don't understand. It's something like those things you made for the Christmas craft sale last year. I spilled coffee on it, and we have to do something before it stains."

Grace smiled her relief that nothing serious had happened to Neil's friend, then frowned as she turned her concentration to the problem at hand. "You have to get at coffee spills right away. Hold on for a second; I have a book. I'll go look it up, but it may take a few minutes."

"That's okay."

Very gently, Grace laid the phone down and hurried into her bedroom to her bookshelf. She ran her finger along the spines of the books, which she had organized into sections by category. She slowed once she found her collection of cookbooks and household hints and tips, then turned her head to read them by title, which she had arranged alphabetically.

In under a minute, the book on stain removal was in her hands, and she returned to the phone.

Cradling the phone on her shoulder, she flipped to the index and rested her finger on the section for coffee stains. "What kind of fabric is it made of?"

Instead of Neil's voice, Phil replied. "It's not cloth. It's made of that white stuff that's thicker than thread but not as thick as string. And it's real stiff. I don't know what it is. I guess it's knitted or something. And underneath the knitted part is some kind of shiny fabric so you can't see through the little holes."

"What color is it? You might have to check for color-fastness."

"White. The whole thing is white. Grace, it's my granny's Christmas angel that we put on top of the tree each year. She's going to be really upset if I've wrecked it. Do you think I can get the coffee out?"

Immediately, Grace knew exactly what he held in his hand. She had patterns for crocheted tree-topper angels in her collection, even though she had not yet attempted one. "That would be crochet cotton and a satin lining." She flipped past the section on carpet stains to the section pertaining to fabrics. "I see no reason why you wouldn't be able to get the coffee out. The book says to use a small amount of a pH-balanced detergent with water, blot it out, and then blot it some more with vinegar and water. It should all come out as long as it's not an old stain."

A silence echoed on the line for a few seconds. "PH-balanced detergent?"

Grace smiled. *Men.* "Use your laundry detergent, as long as it doesn't contain bleach. The label would say if it did."

She could hear the smile in Phil's voice as he spoke. "I just buy the plain stuff, no bleach. That sounds great. First laundry soap, then vinegar. Thanks, Grace. I'd better go do this right away. Sorry to bother you so late. Bye."

Grace barely had time to mumble a quick goodbye, and

Phil was gone. She chatted halfheartedly with Neil for a few minutes, but when neither of them had much to say, they ended the conversation. Grace returned the book to the shelf and picked up the *Heartsong Presents* novel that she had been reading when the phone rang.

She had almost reached the end of the chapter when the buzzer for the door sounded.

Her heart nearly stopped, then began to pound. The clock said nearly midnight. Most of the time, Grace appreciated living in a high-rise apartment building, where she would never be truly alone if she made enough noise, even within the confines of her own apartment. Unfortunately, living in a building with fifteen floors of apartments sometimes meant people pushed the wrong buttons. Or, sometimes kids would randomly push buttons and run, causing trouble in the name of "fun."

Therefore, since she certainly wasn't expecting anyone at this hour, instead of answering the buzzer, she ignored it.

The buzzer sounded again.

Grace's book thudded to the floor. She stared at the phone, and the buzzer sounded a third time. For the first time, she wished that instead of her cat, who was sleeping soundly on the cushion on the other end of the couch, she had a dog, which would be more useful for protection. On the other hand, dogs barked, which was why dogs were not allowed as pets in the apartment building.

With a shaking hand, she picked up the phone and hit the button for the speaker at the door. "Yes?" she asked, trying to keep the tremor out of her voice.

A distorted male voice replied. "Grace? It's me, Phil. I need your help. Sorry to bother you, but I think I made it worse. I can't wait until morning."

She sagged at the relief of hearing a familiar voice, but at the same time, her stomach tied in knots at his obvious distress. "Come on up. I'll see what I can do for you."

While she waited for Phil to come up in the elevator, Grace retrieved her book about stains. She opened the door and stepped into the hallway just as the elevator door opened and Phil stepped out, holding a soggy white lump in his hands. He walked in long, determined steps toward her.

As he approached, she could see his face more clearly with the lessening distance. This was not the Phil she was used to. The Phil she knew was calm, relaxed, always at ease, and always with a ready sense of humor. Even though they were approximately the same age, Phil already showed prominent laugh lines at the corners of his eyes.

Tonight, the only lines showing creased his forehead. His tightly clenched jaw showed no signs of humor, and his posture was so stiff, he seemed taller than usual.

"Come in," she mumbled as she stepped inside.

The door had barely closed behind him when he spoke. "I must have used the wrong kind of soap or done something else wrong. Maybe I used too much vinegar. The coffee came out, like you said, but look what happened to it. The thing collapsed and went all soggy. It's even gotten worse since I left home. Now even the wings went limp. I ruined it, and I don't know what to do. You've got to help me."

He started to hold the angel toward her, but Grace didn't know if she should accept the angel in its present condition, since she couldn't hold it properly with one hand, already occupied with the book.

"Let's take it into the kitchen where the light is better and I can put my book down."

He followed her to the kitchen in silence. Once she laid the book on the table, she carefully accepted the wet, limp lump.

When she turned it over to examine it more fully, the wings flopped over, drooping pathetically. "I don't see any stains, Phil. It looks to me like you got it all out." She didn't mention that she could still smell vinegar, as that could be rinsed out without a problem. Not having to worry about a set stain, Grace relaxed enough to inspect the angel further. What she saw nearly took her breath away. Made of an almost shiny pearl cotton, the angel's wings were intricately crocheted in a complex pattern of what appeared to be mostly a popcorn stitch with perfectly proportioned picots making delicate "feathers" along the bottom rims. The gown was more intricate than anything she'd ever seen before—a combination of rosettes and clusters so close together she didn't know how it stayed flat. Beneath the gown, a cone-shaped satin lining ended inside the angel's head, where Grace suspected the top of the tree was to be inserted to keep the angel perfectly straight.

"This is beautiful, Phil! The craftsmanship is exquisite! Did you say your granny made this?"

"Yes. And if I don't get it fixed up, that same granny is going to kill me. She trusted me with it, and I've let her down. Grace, what am I going to do?"

Grace supported one of the wrinkled wings with her fingers, lifted it, and pulled slightly to test the length. Because it was wet, the cotton slipped from her fingers and flopped down. The two wings came together with a soggy slap. At the mushy sound, Phil winced.

"It's okay, Phil. Really. All we need to do is starch it. When you washed it so nicely to get the coffee out, you also washed the starch out of the gown. The dampness is now seeping into the rest of it, so it's sagging all over as the wetness spreads; after all, it's made of cotton. It will be okay. I just have to wash the whole thing to get all the old starch out, then restarch it. Everything is fine."

His eyes lit up and widened. "Really?"

Grace opened her mouth, but no words came out. She'd never been so close to Neil's friend before. Until this minute, she'd never realized what gorgeous eyes he had. They didn't really seem to be a specific color, they were almost a light smoky gray, tinged a quasi-blue-green. The odd combination made her wonder if his eyes changed color with his mood or a change of clothing. In addition to the color, another attraction was that his eyes were so big and round and very expressive. Throughout her entire conversation with Phil, she could see the interplay of his emotions in his eyes—from desperation at the worry that the angel was ruined, to sadness at knowing he'd been a disappointment to his granny, to shock at the deteriorating condition of the angel, and ending with joy and relief when she told him she could make the angel as good as new.

Grace cleared her throat and turned all her concentration to the angel in her hands, where it should have been in the first place. "Yes. I'm not saying it's going to be easy. I have no idea how to shape something with so many variances, but it's been done before, so it can be done again." Once more, she fingered the wing, then poked at the formerly round head. Since she had no idea what to do, Grace figured it would be better if she did it herself, rather than trying to explain a process of which she wasn't entirely sure. At this point, she didn't even know how much starch to use. "Would you like to leave it with me?"

She couldn't help herself. Grace looked up at Phil. Again, when their eyes met, her breath caught. At her words, his worried expression softened, and a smile began to form. She could see every nuance of the transformation in his eyes and then his entire face. His raised eyebrows lowered and his tight frown relaxed. The corners of his mouth widened and he began to grin. His lips parted slightly at first, and his smile expanded slowly to end with a full, teeth-showing, wide, bright smile—complete with charming laugh lines at the corners of those ladykiller eyes.

"You have no idea what this means to me," he said, his entire face lit up with his smile.

Grace felt like a deer caught in the headlights in that split second before it got run over by a truck. She couldn't tear her gaze away, nor could she find her voice to speak.

Fortunately, Phil tilted his head down as he checked his watch, breaking the direct eye contact. "I guess I'd better go. We've both got to get up for work tomorrow. Thanks again, Grace, and I'm sorry to have bothered you. Give me a call if you need anything or if there's anything I can ever do for you. I don't know how to thank you for this."

She couldn't speak past the tightness in her throat, so she simply nodded and showed him to the door.

The second she locked the door behind him, she pressed her forehead to the cool wood. Phil's muffled footsteps faded into silence as he walked down the hall toward the elevator.

Guilt washed through her as, long after he was gone, she continued to listen to the silence in the hall.

She had no business paying such attention to Phil, regardless of his plight or how fascinating she found his interplay of expression. She wasn't supposed to be interested in anything about Phillip McLean. She was only supposed to be helping Phil fix the damaged angel. Besides, she wasn't doing this for Phil. She was doing this for Neil.

Neil. Whom she'd been dating steadily for the past year. Neil, whom she had recently begun to think was getting ready to ask her if, one day, she might be interested in getting married. Instead of thinking about Phil, she was supposed to be thinking about Neil.

Now, if she could only get the memory of Phil's eyes out of her head.

Chapter 2

Phillip snipped off the price tag and held the stuffed bear in the air. "Do you think she'll like it?"

"Probably," Neil muttered as he flipped through the listing page, then aimed the remote at the television. "I think all women like that kind of stuff."

Phillip sat the little purple bear down on the coffee table. "I don't care about *'all'* women. I just want to know if Grace will like it. What are you doing turning on the television? She told us to be there at seven. It's time to go."

"But the game starts at seven."

Phillip sighed and flopped himself down on the couch. "Come on, Neil. She's doing me a big favor, and you, too. You're the one who splashed coffee all over Granny's angel. I don't want to be rude. She said seven."

"But it's my favorite team. Go without me. I spent the whole evening with Grace yesterday. She knew that I planned to watch the game tonight."

Phillip swiped his fingers through his hair as he stared

at his friend in complete and utter disbelief. The last time he'd had a serious girlfriend, they spent every moment together until the relationship cooled and she dumped him. Since Neil had been going out with Grace for about a year, the excitement of a new relationship was apparently over. Still, Phillip figured that if he had a steady girlfriend, he would much rather spend the time with her than watching a hockey game, regardless of who was playing, at least until the play-offs.

"Come on, Neil. Let's go."

"I said go without me. Grace won't mind. She's probably just going to tell you all about how she fixed your angel. You don't need me for that."

Phillip opened his mouth, about to tell Neil that if that were the case, then he could watch the game just as well from Grace's couch as from their own, but he stopped short. Since Neil and Grace had started going together, Phillip hadn't been able to understand their relationship. Therefore, he wasn't likely to figure it out today.

"Fine," he snapped, not at all trying to keep the edge of sarcasm out of his voice. "Is there a message or anything you want me to pass on?"

"Naw. See you later." Without waiting for a response, Neil turned up the volume on the television.

Phillip ground his teeth, feeling thoroughly dismissed. He left without another word.

On the drive to Grace's apartment, his thoughts quickly changed from Neil and Grace's relationship to Granny's angel. By the time he buzzed Grace's apartment and traveled up the elevator, he could hardly wait to see the angel restored to its former state so Granny would never know the disaster that had befallen it.

The same as his previous visit, Grace stood in the hallway outside her apartment door, waiting for him as he walked out of the elevator.

Her brows knotted as she watched the elevator door close behind him. "Where's Neil?"

"Uh, he was…busy," Phillip muttered, not at all appreciating the position Neil had placed him in. He forced himself to smile. "How's the angel?" He held out the little stuffed bear he'd bought for her. "Here."

Very slowly, she accepted his gift. "Thank you. What is this for?"

"It's just a little something to thank you for helping me with the angel and especially for putting up with me when I barged in on you like that. Neil said you'd like it."

The second his words left his mouth, Phillip mentally kicked himself. He'd only meant to put in a good word for Neil. Instead, all he accomplished was to, again, draw Grace's attention to Neil's absence.

Her cheeks turned a cute shade of pink. "That was very nice of you, but your thanks might be a little premature. Come in and I'll show you."

Phillip's heart sank. He followed her into the kitchen, where the angel lay on the table, even more limp and shriveled than the way he left it. The only difference was, today, it was dry.

Grace slid the angel toward him, but he didn't dare touch it.

"I washed your angel again to get all the old starch out, but restarching it is going to be more work than I originally anticipated, so I stopped. Let me show you why. See the lining?" Leaving the angel on the table, Grace turned up the edge of the gown to show him where the lining joined the crocheted outer shell.

"The crochet cotton is going to require a very heavy-duty dose of starch to make it stiff enough to stand unassisted. At the same time, the lining has to be pliant enough to mold to the shape of the tree branch underneath. That means I have to take the satin lining off and starch just the crochet cotton, then sew it back on when the angel is dry. The same with the hair and the halo."

Phillip stared at the angel. While he didn't know Grace tremendously well, he knew both from various social activities at the church and from things Neil said that Grace was quite proficient at handicrafts. He hadn't taken much notice of Grace before Neil started dating her, but since then, whenever her name came up, because of her association with Neil, he paid attention. On occasion, even his granny had mentioned Grace's proficiency and talents with the items she donated to the fund-raisers and craft bazaars, which was high praise, indeed.

If Grace anticipated difficulty in restoring the angel, then he didn't know whom else to turn to.

Phillip gulped. Hesitantly, he turned toward Grace. "Does this mean you can't do it?"

Grace shook her head. "No, no. I think I can do it, just it's not going to be easy. The hard part is going to be getting the angel to dry in the right shape. When I starch doilies, I use cardboard with a dish towel over top, then stretch the doily out with pins and wait for it to dry. I can't do that with the angel because it's so oddly shaped. The body is cone shaped, the head is round like a ball, the wings are flat, and the arms are tubes bent at a forty-five-degree angle. I haven't yet been able to figure out how to contour all the different pieces at the same time until it's dry, but obviously it can be done. That's why I called you over, to see if we could put our heads together and come up with some ideas."

Phillip blinked and stared blankly at the bedraggled angel. Because he was familiar with the angel, he knew what it was supposed to look like, which was nothing like its present condition. Looking at it like this was almost painful. "Can't we do it one section at a time?"

"No. Remember what happened when you wet one section to wash it? The dampness seeped into the whole thing, and it went limp one section at a time. The angel is large. I know you don't think it can be considered heavy, but it is when it's wet, especially when you realize that it's just made of thick, cotton thread. It's got to support its own weight, which is a tall order for something so elaborate. Spray starch would never hold it. It needs to be starched the old-fashioned way, which means soaking it thoroughly. That means we have to figure out how to dry it into shape."

Cautiously, he lifted one delicate white arm, then a limp wing, analyzing the various components and the construction of the angel as a whole. Pangs of guilt began to gnaw at Phillip as he began to realize the magnitude of what he had asked Grace to do. At the same time, tiny fingers of anger began to poke at him. The person absent and doing nothing was the person who was at fault.

He shook the thought from his mind and forced his concentration on the angel's former appearance. Fair or not, he needed Grace to help him restore the angel, aside from the amount of effort required. He would deal with Neil later. Regardless of his growing anger, it wasn't right to seek retribution. That was God's job, although in this case, unnecessary, because, after all, it was just an accident. Phillip only wanted to have the angel back to the way it was supposed to be.

"I guess that means building a framework or something."

"Probably. Do you know how your granny did it?"

"I don't have a clue. I don't want to ask her either, because if I do, she's going to know something is wrong. My first thought is to put together some kind of support structure from underneath."

Grace nodded and pressed her lips together so one corner of her mouth pointed downward. All thoughts of planning a structure deserted Phillip as he watched the interplay of thought on Grace's face as she concentrated on the possibilities.

"Yes," she mumbled, nodding as she spoke. "That would be first. We need something cone shaped."

Phillip shook his head to get his thoughts where they should have been in the first place, which was not being amused by the cute way Grace scrunched her eyebrows. "We also need a cross section to brace and support the wings, yet keep them flat. I don't know what we can do about the head and arms...."

Together they discussed various ways to fashion a frame and decided, for lack of a practical solution, that a trip to the hardware store might spark some workable ideas.

Being Thursday evening, the store was open until nine, giving them opportunity to go while their ideas were fresh.

Oddly, once inside the store, Phillip discovered Grace was relatively comfortable around the tools and hardware. Even though she didn't know the names of most of the common tools, she knew what they were for, which he found strangely refreshing. To his surprise, she knew the most about hot-melt glue guns. Phillip discovered she even owned one when she picked up a box of glue sticks to replenish her stock.

Slowly, they made their way through the tools, through the hardware and plumbing sections, and into the aisle for drapery hardware and fixtures. Eventually they found themselves in the end-of-the-season clearance section for yard and gardening supplies, still empty-handed.

Absently, Phillip ran his fingers over the cut edge of a marked-down spool of previously opened wire mesh that was sitting at the edge of the table. "I don't know what we're going to do. I can't think of anything," he mumbled, thinking out loud more than expecting to make conversation. Slowly, he ran his fingers over the cut edge of the reel, absently bending the wire as he spoke. "I have a bad feeling I'm going to have to ask Granny after all."

"Chicken wire!"

Grace's sudden exclamation caused him to jump, nearly knocking the spool off the table.

He turned to Grace, who grabbed the spool before it rolled away.

"This is great!" she exclaimed as she ran her fingers over the wire mesh, which was about a foot wide. "We could use this chicken wire to shape everything!" With her raised voice, a few people turned to stare. Grace's cheeks turned a cute shade of pink, and she lowered her voice. "We can bend it into a cone, make tubes for the arms, and make a flat piece to stretch out and keep the wings straight. We can do everything except make it round enough to shape the head."

"Chicken wire?" Phillip muttered, trying to imagine how to bend chicken wire with any amount of precision. The angel was only ten inches tall, and the arms were no bigger than his index fingers. The only way he could figure out how to obtain the correct shape and size would be a slow and painful process involving needle-nosed pliers, bending the mesh one frame at a time.

Grace's face lit up, and she raised one finger in the air. "Oh! A balloon! Remember back in kindergarten, making papier-mâché animals? We can do the same thing, only on a smaller scale. We can use a balloon inside the head."

Once again, the same people turned to stare. This time, Grace ignored them.

All Phillip could do was stare at the spool. Personally, he couldn't see that her idea would work. However, he'd asked for Grace's help and therefore had to accept what she suggested. He reminded himself that her reputation for making crafts preceded her—even Granny was impressed with Grace's handicrafts. To boost his confidence that they really could fix the angel, Phillip envisioned the angel, restored and perfect, sitting atop his parents' tree on Christmas morning.

Phillip looked upward to the signs suspended from the ceiling summarizing the contents of that aisle. "Do you think they sell balloons here?"

"I have no idea. Let's find out."

Without waiting for him, suddenly Grace walked away. Quickly, Phillip grabbed the spool and hurried after her.

When he caught up to her, he turned down the first aisle, expecting Grace to join him so they could begin their search. After a few steps, when he realized Grace had gone straight and wasn't with him, he spun on his toes and quickened his pace to catch up to her on the center walkway.

"Where are you going?"

She pointed to the center of the store without replying and kept walking, straight to the customer-service counter.

"Pardon me," she said to the young clerk behind the counter. "Do you sell balloons here? Not regular party balloons, but the smaller ones. The kind used for water fights."

The girl's eyebrows rose as she glanced briefly at Phillip, cleared her throat, then turned her attention back to Grace. Phillip grinned weakly, then backed up a step.

"I'm sorry," the girl said cheerfully. "We don't carry water-fight balloons here. We don't carry any kind of balloons."

The second Grace mumbled a quick thank-you, Phillip turned and headed for the checkouts. Once they were waiting in line, he leaned toward her, keeping his voice low. "What are you doing, asking for water balloons? Did you see the look she gave me? She must have thought we were crazy, thinking of water fights when it's freezing outside."

They shuffled forward in the line. "I wasn't about to

explain to her why we needed a small balloon. I know the discount megastore would have balloons, although I don't know if they'd have the ones we need, especially this time of year. At this point, I'm ready to buy any kind of balloon. They should still be open. Want to go there on the way home?"

Phillip checked his watch. "I guess. The sooner we can get the angel fixed and back to normal, the better."

He paid for the wire in silence, then listened to Grace talk about other projects she'd made for church bazaars over the years during the drive.

Unlike the hardware store, the megastore was crowded. However, this time women made up the majority of the clientele.

"I've never been here before. This place is huge," Phillip mumbled as he glanced around the warehouse-size store. "I think I need some groceries. Since we're here, do you mind if I pick up a few things?"

Grace checked her watch. "I don't mind, but let's get the balloons first so we don't forget or run out of time."

Usually Phillip shopped for groceries at the neighborhood store, buying things when he needed them. He didn't remember the prices of much that he bought, but it seemed, just as he'd heard, the superstore prices were lower. The only disadvantage was having to buy everything in large quantities. However, since he knew he was saving money in the long run, every time he saw something he knew he would use, he added it to the growing pile in his buggy.

Every time he added an item, Grace quirked one eyebrow, but she said nothing until he added a flat of large economy-size chocolate muffins.

"I can't believe you. Do you really think you and Neil are going to eat all those before they get stale?"

"The lady said they kept well in the freezer."

Grace rolled her eyes but made no further comment as they continued walking.

The moment they arrived at the checkout, Phillip began to unload everything onto the conveyor belt, while Grace stood in front of him, watching everything go by. When he had the last item up on the belt, he reached into his back pocket for his wallet, and joined her.

She never stopped watching his groceries, as the clerk dragged each item over the scanner, then placed the scanned items into the second buggy. "I can't believe everything you bought. In addition to all the cans and boxes, you have a whole case of frozen juice, a package of three roasts that you're going to have to repackage before you freeze them, and this big bag of buns will have to go in the freezer, as well as that five-gallon tub of ice cream. I'm going to assume you don't have a chest freezer, only the one in the top part of the fridge. Just how much do you think you're going to stuff in there?"

"Uh... Maybe Neil and I are going to have to eat a lot of chocolate muffins in the next few days. Would you like to have a couple?"

"I think you're missing my point. I came for balloons, and I'm leaving with balloons, milk, and bread." She swept one hand in the air to encompass all his purchases. "Just how much cash do you carry around for impulse purchases?"

Phillip removed his bankcard from his wallet, tipped his head, and waved the card back and forth between them a few times. "That's what these are for."

Grace shook her head. "You're going to need a bank loan to pay for everything you've got here."

All Phillip could do was grin.

By the time they had all the groceries packed into the car and he had Grace back home, it was late. Instead of figuring out exactly how they would construct the frame to support the angel while it dried, he merely carried her bag of groceries up the elevator and saw Grace safely inside her apartment.

"I hate to keep bothering you. This has turned into so much more than I envisioned. Are you busy tomorrow? I have a feeling that what we have to build is going to take a long time."

Grace nodded. "Yes, I have a feeling you're right. Neil and I were going to get together tomorrow because it's Friday, but we don't have specific plans. Maybe we can all stay here and build a framework together, since it's Neil's fault this happened in the first place."

Phillip didn't want to go there. He had caught himself getting annoyed with Neil a few times in the course of the evening, since he was the one doing all the work and running around and Neil was at home enjoying the hockey game. Still, he was glad Grace said it and not him.

"Great, I'll see you tomorrow night. With Neil. By the way, I put a couple of those chocolate muffins in the bag with your bread. Enjoy."

Chapter 3

Grace set the grocery bag containing the cornstarch onto the kitchen table and glanced at the clock on the stove. Fortunately she had made it home before Neil and Phil's arrival, but she didn't have too much time before they were due.

She couldn't believe that she'd just been shopping the day before, the sole purpose being to buy the means with which to support the angel after they starched it, and had forgotten the starch.

The only reason she could think of was that she had allowed herself to become distracted.

Even though she'd talked to Phil countless times since she started dating Neil, she hadn't paid much attention to him. Of course she thought Phil was nice. After all, he was Neil's best friend. If Neil liked him, it seemed only natural that she would like him, too. However, she'd never before found him so distracting.

Grace started a pot of coffee, then walked into the liv-

ing room. As she reached for the book she had been reading the night before, she spotted the little stuffed bear Phil
had given her. Instead of picking up the book, she picked
up the bear.

She patted the little bear on the head and smiled. When
Phil said he had given it to her just to thank her for her
help in restoring the angel's shape, she couldn't help but
appreciate the gesture. While it wasn't exactly for no reason, Grace certainly hadn't expected, nor wanted, anything
in return for helping him. Even without their mutual relationship with Neil, Grace would gladly have helped Phil,
or anyone, if asked.

Her smile widened as she thought of Phil actually buying the bear. If Phil had been embarrassed when she asked
the clerk at the hardware store for water balloons, she
couldn't imagine him buying a purple bear, yet he obviously had. His effort made her appreciate his gift all the
more. She found his small gift strangely touching, but
forced herself to shrug it off, telling herself that she was
only so fascinated by it because no one had ever given her
such a silly little gift before.

Rather than think too much about the bear, Grace replaced it to its position of honor on the mantel. Knowing
Neil was always late, she sat on the couch and reached for
her book, intending to finish the chapter she'd been interrupted from reading.

She had no sooner picked up the book when the buzzer
for the door sounded. As usual, once she pushed the button to open the main door, Grace waited in the hallway
outside her door. Neil and Phil stepped out of the elevator
at the same time, each holding a bag.

"Hi," both men chorused in unison, smiling as they
approached.

Grace felt herself blushing at receiving the attention of
two men, something she was not used to.

She cleared her throat. "We'd better get right to work. I'm still not sure what we're doing. Three heads are definitely going to be better than one."

Once in the kitchen, both men emptied their respective bags onto the table. Phil's bag contained the spool of wire mesh, a haphazard bundle of some kind of thin, plastic-coated wire, and the balloons. Neil's bag contained an assortment of hand tools. Grace retrieved the angel, her hair, halo, and lining already removed, and they all sat.

She assigned Neil to cut and mold the cone shape to support the body. Phil cut the flat pieces for the wings, then began the excruciating task of fashioning two wire-mesh tubes for the arms. Both men grumbled when she inserted a balloon into the angel's head and blew it up, then announced that her part of the framework was done.

Even though she had told Phil about her idea to insert the balloon, when he saw it done, he came up with the idea to insert two of the tube-shaped balloons into the arms and build wire-mesh tubes in the right size, then shape them to fit around the exterior of the arms. He insisted they would be easier to remove later. Of course, Grace agreed, making sure to compliment Phil for his good idea.

As the men worked at their respective tasks, Grace mixed the cornstarch and water and proceeded to cook it, stirring carefully during the entire process.

Once the liquid cleared and thickened, Grace removed the saucepan from the stove and continued to stir as the mixture cooled.

While she stirred, she watched the two men, who were now nearly finished.

When the ladies' group from church gathered together to do crafts, laughter and endless chatter always accompanied their activities. Their craft sessions had become as much a social gathering as an opportunity to assemble the items that would be donated to the bazaars and fund-raisers. On the other hand, during the entire time she worked with Neil and Phil, she could count the number of sentences the men had exchanged on one hand.

The men were silent for so long that Neil's, "We're done," caused her to drop the spoon into the pot.

She tried not to show her embarrassment as she fished out the slippery spoon with another spoon. Most of all, she hoped they wouldn't laugh. "I think this is almost cool enough to work with. We just need to put everything in place, and we're ready to starch her. Have you finished positioning the arms?"

"Almost," Phil mumbled.

Grace continued to stir the mixture slowly, but instead of concentrating on the cooling starch mixture, she watched Phil. Since she already enjoyed working with crafts, Grace was well accustomed to the delicate handling required with such finely detailed projects. Nothing she had done had been a surprise, although the work had gone slowly. Now, watching Phil with his large hands working on the delicate components, she couldn't tear her gaze away. She could see his obvious struggles to insert the balloons properly into the angel's arms, which were smaller than his fingers, and around the angel's body, which he had halfway inside out. Part of her wanted to relieve him and do it herself, yet something told her that more significant than his difficulties, he felt it important to do it himself.

Once he blew up the balloons to round out the arms, he very gently returned the gown to the correct position. Then, he set to work covering the inflated arms with small mesh pieces using needle-nosed pliers, making sure the arms were properly bent at the elbows. Once the arms were covered, he gave the angel to Neil, who inserted the cone up into the angel's gown until it was fitted snugly.

Grace reached for the flat mesh sections that were to support the wings, then froze. "I just thought of something. We can't put the frame over the wings because of the breadth of the span. We're going to have to starch her first. Here goes."

Holding her breath, Grace mentally said a quick prayer for success and mumbled a quick "amen" not loud enough for Neil and Phil to hear. Before another doubt that she wasn't doing it right plagued her, in one quick motion, Grace submerged the angel into the lukewarm liquid starch mixture.

"What are you doing!?" Phil called out at the same time as he jumped to his feet.

Neil's horrified expression mirrored Phil's, only Neil remained seated.

Her hands froze in the pot, up to her wrists in the lukewarm liquid. "I'm starching the angel."

"But you dunked it. You've got it all wet again."

"Of course I've gotten it all wet. What did you think I was going to do with that stuff I've been cooking?"

Phil ran his fingers through his hair. "I don't know. I thought you were going to paint it on or something."

Grace blinked and stared at Phil, whose face had gone very pale. "But I have to make sure every section is completely saturated. I don't know any other way to do it. This is how I starch doilies."

His face regained a little color, but not much. "Sorry. I know you know what you're doing. But a vision of how soggy and floppy the angel got after I washed it flashed through my mind. It wasn't pretty."

She forced herself to smile, not willing to admit that while she had done this procedure often with doilies, she'd never done it with a shaped object. Grace told herself that even if what she was now doing didn't work, all she had to do was wash the starch out, and the condition of the angel would be no different than when she first laid hands on it. "If it would make you feel better, you can do it yourself.

It's not difficult, and it's just cornstarch and water. There's nothing here that could possibly cause any damage."

Phil shook his head and sank into his chair. "That's okay. I'll just watch. Sorry."

Grace kept the angel submersed as she spoke. "How about if I tell you what I'm doing as I'm doing it?" When neither Phil nor Neil responded, Grace continued anyway. "I'm now going to make sure the starch mixture is soaked into every part." Using her index finger, she poked and prodded the angel to encourage the cotton threads to absorb the starch mixture. She tried not to look at Phil, who cringed with every poke to his precious angel.

"And now I'm making sure the wings have a good dose of starch, because they have to be very stiff to maintain that straight shape out to the sides. This is what I do for doilies. They end up flat, just like the wings will be." Using both hands, she wrung the wings as if they were a dishcloth, then gently tugged on them while still submerged to make sure they soaked in as much starch mixture as possible. When she squeezed the wings a second time, she didn't dare look at Phil.

"Done." After lifting the angel out of the starch mixture, Grace once more wrung out the wings. She then ran her fingers over every surface of the angel akin to a windshield-wiper blade, pressing out the excess visible starch. With every swipe, gooey blobs dripped into the saucepan, landing with a solid plop rather than a splash, as the mixture had already become quite thick.

"That's disgusting," Neil mumbled.

Grace forced herself to smile. "It's a little slimy, but it's not bad once you get used to it. Kind of like finger paint. Now if it were raw egg, *that* would be disgusting."

Phil smiled, big and wide. Momentarily, Grace's hands froze. Apparently all Phil's worries were forgotten, at least for the moment, which was more than she could say for herself.

"You're right," he said, not losing his smile. "That stuff does look awful slimy, though. I really appreciate you doing this for me."

"Yeah, Grace. Me, too," added Neil. "Especially since this is all my fault."

When she first committed herself to restoring the angel, Grace had compared the project to a scaled-down craft session with the ladies from church. However, the project had turned into nothing like an outing with the ladies. Being constantly watched and her actions scrutinized when she wasn't entirely sure of what she was doing only made her self-conscious of every possible mistake she could make. All she could think of to justify herself was to keep repeating in her head that she was doing the best she could with the available resources.

"Accidents happen," she mumbled. "Pretty soon it will be as good as new, maybe better, because we don't know the last time she's been washed since this is such an involved process. Let's get the wings flattened, and then all we have to do is let her dry."

They worked together in silence. Neil held the flat piece of mesh in place while Grace flattened and stretched out one wet wing on top of the piece Neil held flat. Then, while she held the wing outstretched over the top of the mesh, Phil pressed the second piece of mesh over the top, sandwiching the wing between the two pieces. After repeating the procedure for the second wing, the two men lifted the angel to stand upright, holding everything in place while Grace used the plastic-coated wire to bind the mesh together tightly so the wings would stay upright in position and firmly supported while they dried. Neil made sure the mesh would remain stretched out by fastening pieces of wood to the back of the sections of mesh.

Next, Grace inserted plastic straws through the bottom, up through the mesh cone, to support the head and keep it from tipping to one side while it was wet.

Very carefully, they supported the angel trapped within all the pieces of the frame with chopsticks and piles of books, repositioning every part of the angel and support network until everything was perfect.

With crossed arms, all three of them stood back to admire their finished project.

Phil spoke first. "If I didn't know what Granny's angel looked like before all this happened, I wouldn't be able to tell now. You can hardly see it through all this stuff."

Grace nodded. "I know what you mean. She looks rather strange with all the wire and mesh everywhere, especially with all the chopsticks sticking all over the place. Not only that, I'm sure she'll look much better and more like normal when we put her hair and the halo back on. She looks rather ugly bald, doesn't she?"

Phil turned to her. "Since when did you start referring to Granny's angel as a *she?* I don't know why angels are always portrayed as women, especially at Christmastime. In every instance in the Bible where an angel came down to pay mankind a visit and deliver a message, angels were always seen as men."

Grace knit her brows as she stared intently at the obviously female, albeit hairless, angel propped up on her kitchen table. "They were? Are you sure?"

"Yup. I've always felt strange about the female angels that are shown everywhere at Christmas, but when I start seeing the baby cherub kind of angels, I start to get annoyed. That's plain old wrong."

Grace blinked and stared at him. "So what if every instance of an angel appearing before mankind in the Bible was male? That doesn't mean that showing angels as anything else is necessarily wrong."

"If it's not right, then it's wrong, Grace. Could it be any other way?"

"But sometimes there are gray areas. In fact, in most cases in life, there isn't necessarily a right or wrong answer."

Phil crossed his arms. "I disagree. There's always a bottom line, just most of the time, people aren't willing to go there. It's like being pregnant. You are or you aren't, and when it comes down to the final answer, there is nothing in between."

Grace's cheeks burned at his choice of examples. "Well…" she sputtered and let her voice trail off as she realized that arguing with Phil was pointless, at least on this issue. Or, at least until she did some research on the matter. "Let's change the subject. *The angel,*" she emphasized the gender-neutral description, "should be dry in a couple of days, which brings us to Sunday. I don't think it's a good idea for me to deliver it to you at church because then your granny will be wondering why I had it in the first place. Why don't the two of you come over after church, and I'll make lunch?" She glanced back and forth between the two men.

Neil's face lit up. "Yeah! That sounds great." He turned to Phil. "Grace makes a great ham-and-cheese omelet. You're going to love it. It's to die for."

Instead of the smile she expected from Phil, he stiffened from head to foot and crossed his arms over his chest. The happy-go-lucky gray-green of his eyes she had so admired only the day before turned to a steel, icy blue-gray as Phil stared at Neil. "I have a better idea," he said, his voice rather low-pitched and perfectly even. "Since Grace is going through all this work and taking all this time to help us, I think we should take her to Farley's Cafe after church, and we'll *buy* her a ham-and-cheese omelet. Or better yet, *you* can pay."

A heavy silence hung in the air.

"Uh…I guess…" Neil muttered, then stood. "I think we'd better be going. Remember, Phil, we have to get up early tomorrow to be at your granny's because she's giving us—uh, I mean, you—that couch."

Grace opened her mouth, about to comment on Neil willingly being early for something, but snapped it shut before she said anything. If they were alone, she would have teased him, but it wasn't right to do so in front of Phil. Besides, Phil and Neil had been living together for a number of years. If anyone knew how Neil was consistently late, it would be Phil. They didn't need to gang up on Neil. Even though his constant disregard for the importance of being on time continually grated on her nerves, Grace had decided to learn to live with it. She doubted she would ever change him. Any attempts to do so would be a waste of energy.

As well, the possibility existed that Phil was equally as bad, making it doubly pointless to challenge Neil about habitual tardiness. Although, the more Grace thought about it, Phil had been early the evening they ended up going shopping, and the two of them had arrived in plenty of time to get the angel done tonight.

She saw them to the door, then stood in the hall until the elevator door closed behind them.

Grace quietly walked back into her apartment, wondering what Sunday would bring.

"Bye, Granny! Thanks again for everything!" Phillip called out the passenger-side window.

Neil leaned out the driver's window at the same time. "Yeah. Thanks, Mrs. McLean."

Phillip watched Granny wave back. "You're welcome, dear. It's my pleasure, and I'm more than happy to be able to give all those things to people who need them."

With one last wave, Neil shifted into first gear and began the drive home.

Neil and Phillip yawned at the same time.

Phillip smiled in the middle of his yawn, but didn't bother to cover his mouth with his hand. Not only was he just with Neil, but even if he wasn't, he was too tired to care. "Thanks for all your help, Neil. I had no idea this was going to turn into an all-day moving party. Granny gave away a lot of stuff to a lot of people. I didn't know that you'd be the only one here who owns a pickup truck."

Neil smiled and nodded, not taking his attention off his driving. "No problem. I don't mind at all, although I think we're both going to be stiff tomorrow. If it was earlier, I'd think of paying a surprise visit to Grace. Did you know she's got a hot tub and a sauna in that apartment building she lives in?"

Phillip lost his smile. All day long, even though all they'd done was move furniture and appliances of all shapes and sizes and weights, so many things had reminded him of Grace. When they moved Granny's old chest freezer to his cousin Trevor's house, he remembered Grace's teasing comments about the chocolate muffins that never did make it into the freezer. All through Granny's house he'd seen handmade ornaments. Seeing Granny's doilies doubly reminded him of Grace, especially when he'd noticed a doily on Granny's coffee table very similar to a smaller one he'd seen at Grace's place.

Of course it hadn't helped when Granny herself mentioned Grace outright. At the time she was speaking to Neil about the possibilities of giving away some of her crafting supplies. Granny had said that of all the younger ladies in the church, Grace was the one who would likely make the most use of her extra knitting needles. Granny had discovered that when she started to sort and pack her things, she often found two, and even three, pairs of the same sizes.

Phillip crossed his arms over his chest and leaned back in the seat as Neil stopped for a red light. "Speaking of Grace, I hope you remember that we're taking her out for lunch tomorrow after church."

Neil's brows knotted. "Of course I remember. We usually spend Sunday afternoons together. Sometimes we go out, sometimes we go back to her place, and sometimes she comes over to our place, but that depends if you're home."

"I don't remember you bringing her to our place on Sundays. Now that you mention it, she hardly ever comes over to our place."

Neil nodded. "That's because I know most of the time when you're going to be home."

Phillip clenched his jaw as he considered the ramifications of Neil's statement. He hadn't known that the reason he didn't see much of Grace was because Neil purposely avoided him. Part of him could understand that, in most cases, the third person often felt the odd man out. In such a case, Neil had been avoiding bringing Grace to their home to spare him the potential for discomfort. However, another part of him was oddly annoyed, and he didn't know why.

Now that he thought about it, and since he'd had an opportunity to spend some time with Grace, Phillip realized that he wanted to get to know her better. Of course she was Neil's girlfriend. Naturally, Phillip respected that relationship. Still, that didn't stop Phillip from wanting to be just plain old ordinary friends with Grace. Many people developed and maintained platonic friendships with someone of opposite gender.

He cleared his throat. "You don't have to worry if I'm home or not. I don't mind you bringing Grace over. If you don't mind me sharing the living room with the two of you, that's okay with me. We don't all always have to stay in the living room either. There's the kitchen, and the backyard in the summertime, too, you know. There's plenty of room for everyone."

"You don't mind? That's great. Maybe I will bring Grace over more often, especially when summertime comes. I know she likes to sit outside in the fresh air, but living in an apartment doesn't give her much chance to do that. It's not the same sitting in the backyard as sitting on the eleventh-floor balcony. Did you know that she's not allowed to barbecue things on her balcony? They say it's a potential fire hazard to the balcony above."

"That makes sense. No, I don't mind. Maybe that will give us an excuse to try barbecuing something other than hamburgers and hot dogs next year."

Neil grinned from ear to ear as they pulled up to their house and he shifted the truck into park. "Yeah. We can impress her with our great teamwork. I'll light the barbecue, you can cook the steaks, and I'll supervise."

Phillip grinned. "Nice try, Neil."

Neil grinned back. "I couldn't help it."

Despite Neil's attempt to get out of his turns at cooking, Phillip now looked forward to future Sundays more than ever. But, for the coming Sunday, they were scheduled to end up at Grace's apartment. And he could hardly wait.

Chapter 4

"God bless you, and go in the peace of Christ."

"Amen," the congregation replied in almost-unison.

The pastor stepped away from the podium, and people began to shuffle away from their seats as the sanctuary slowly emptied into the foyer.

Fortunately for Phillip, once he arrived in the foyer, many of the grateful recipients of Granny's excess furniture flocked around her, again thanking her for everything she'd given away. This gave Phillip a good excuse not to join in and thank her, too, as he was positive the topic of her treasured angel would come up in conversation. Even though, by now, the angel would be back to normal, Phillip wasn't yet ready to tell her about what happened or the lengths he and Neil and Grace had gone through to fix it. He doubted he ever would.

He turned back to the people in his small group when Neil poked him in the ribs. "Come on, Phil. If we don't get out of here fast, we'll have to wait for a table."

Phillip didn't need to be asked twice. Immediately he excused himself and headed with Neil and Grace toward the exit. Still, he had to comment. "Don't rush me. Remember, you have to be nice to me since we're using my car."

Neil snorted. "We didn't have to come in your car. Three people can fit in my pickup quite easily."

"Which doesn't negate the fact that it's still my car, I'm the driver, and you still have to be nice to me."

"I'll be nice to you when you give me back that CD you borrowed last month."

"I didn't borrow it. We traded. That means you've got one of mine, and you've got to give it back first."

"Boys!" Grace interjected. "Are you two always like this?"

"No," said Phillip, grinning widely.

"Yes," mumbled Neil.

The cold wind hit them as soon as they stepped outside the shelter of the building. Phillip mentally kicked himself for not choosing a warmer jacket and quickened his pace.

When he was close enough to his car, he aimed the remote control on his key chain. He hit the switch to unlock the doors and immediately shuffled around to the driver's side. Just as he touched the handle, Phillip paused. If he had been alone with Grace, he would have opened the car door for her, like he had when they went shopping together. However, this time, even though they were together as a group, she wasn't really with him. Grace really was with Neil.

Instead of getting into the car first, he waited. A flicker of satisfaction passed through him when Neil opened the door for Grace and waited for her to slide in.

As soon as Grace positioned herself in the center of the front seat, Phillip slid in beside her.

"I'll have you know that there would have been more room in my pickup than having the three of us squashed in like sardines," Neil grumbled as he slid into the passenger side of the front seat on the other side of Grace.

Phillip opened his mouth to give Neil a rebuttal, but nothing came out. This time, Neil was correct. If the threesome had consisted of three men, they would have thought nothing of one of them sitting alone in the backseat. But such was not the case. Technically Neil was with Grace, so the two of them would naturally sit together. However, Phillip would have felt awkward to have Neil and Grace in the back, while he was alone in the front to drive. If Neil sat alone in the backseat, that would have left Phillip in the front with Grace, which wasn't proper. Grace was Neil's date, even though they had only attended the Sunday morning service. Grace sitting alone in the backseat was not a consideration.

Phillip had never been part of a threesome where one of the three was female. He was discovering the hard way that things he'd never thought about before had suddenly become complicated.

Grace's voice broke the silence. "We're not that squished, and don't worry about it, Phil. This way is warmer. I've also noticed that since your car is smaller, it heats up faster than Neil's truck."

Phillip smiled while Neil grumbled a comment he likely didn't want to hear. Until the thin layer of frost cleared from the windshield, they chatted about the morning's service; then Phillip drove to the pancake restaurant.

At first Phillip wasn't sure how he would fit into the conversation, being an obvious third person, but once the dialogue got going, he couldn't remember the last time he'd had such fun at lunch after church. Between the three of them, talking never stopped. The only time they slowed was to pray over their food when it was served.

Conversation still flowed all the way to the car and during the drive back to Grace's apartment.

As they neared Grace's apartment, Phillip's thoughts returned to the angel—the reason they all had come together in the first place. In a way, he was almost sorry the angel was all fixed. Now he had no reason to see Grace. His only consolation was that he had opened up the door to Neil's having Grace over to their home more frequently, despite the fact that Phillip would tend to be the odd man out.

Only once they stood in the elevator did Phillip notice a change in Grace. As the elevator rose, Grace became increasingly quiet. If not for her growing grin, worry might have started to set in. But, because of the grin, he found his own excitement growing at the thought of seeing his recovered angel.

Grace opened the apartment door and stood back, allowing him to enter first. Without needing to be told where to go, Phillip headed straight for the kitchen.

His breath caught at the sight of Granny's angel, fully restored to its former beauty, sitting in the center of Grace's kitchen table. Not only had Grace removed all the supports, but she'd also replaced the hair and the halo, and sewn the lining back in.

"It's beautiful!" he gasped as he picked the angel up. Very gently, he ran his fingertips over the top of one wing, barely able to believe the transformation from the soggy lump of only three days before. "I don't know what to say." His hand froze when he reached the tip of the wing. Even though the angel looked exactly like it had on the day he brought it home, Phillip had never known the process or what was involved in making something made of thread stand up by itself or how the wings were made to extend so gracefully to the sides. Now that he knew, he appreciated the beauty and craftsmanship of the angel even more. And in so doing, he appreciated even more how Grace had so willingly offered to help when she knew the extent of the time and energy involved when he hadn't.

He looked up at Grace, staring deeply into her big brown eyes. "A simple thank-you doesn't seem like enough."

At first she smiled, but then her face turned ten shades of red and she looked down at the floor. "You're welcome," she mumbled. She let a short silence hang and then checked her watch. "I don't mean to kick you guys out, but I'm expected over at my sister's for dinner. I have to get ready, and I don't want to arrive just before she's ready to put everything on the table."

Phillip nodded and held the angel closer to his body. "No problem; I understand. Thank you again, Grace. For everything."

Not wanting to create an awkward situation, Phillip walked out of the kitchen in case Neil wanted to kiss her goodbye. And, not wanting to listen to Neil kiss Grace, Phillip continued walking once he reached the hall and made his way all the way to the apartment's main door.

To his surprise, when he turned around, Neil was already behind him, and Grace was behind Neil. They exchanged a quick, kissless goodbye. Phillip and Neil stepped into the hall toward the elevator, and the door closed behind them.

As soon as they were in the privacy of the elevator, Phillip could no longer keep quiet.

He turned to Neil. "I know it's probably none of my business, but you've been dating Grace for about a year now. What's going on? You didn't kiss her goodbye. In fact, I don't remember you kissing her goodbye on Thursday evening either. Are you two on the outs or something?"

Neil turned his head toward Phil, his eyebrows knotted in the middle of his forehead. "On the outs? No. What makes you say that?"

Phillip ran his fingers through his hair. "I don't know. You two just don't seem, well, romantic or anything. You act like an old couple who's been together for fifty years or something. But even my granny and grampa kissed good-bye and stuff up until the day he died."

"Grace is shy. I respect that."

Phillip remained silent to let Neil's words sink in. He hadn't considered Grace to be shy before, but now that Neil mentioned it, he could remember a few times when he'd made very pointed and direct eye contact with Grace. She wouldn't look him in the eye. Instead, both times she blushed and turned away. Yet, he couldn't equate her behavior with him with her actions at the hardware store.

Phillip would have been content to simply walk up and down the aisles until he found, or didn't find, what they were seeking. Conversely, Grace had boldly marched straight to the service counter. She hadn't cared that the clerk looked at them strangely, obviously finding it amusing that two supposed adults were asking for water balloons when there was snow on the ground. The clerk's amusement at their request had gone right over Grace's head, but Phillip had been quite embarrassed. Because of her reaction at the time, Phillip would never have considered that Grace might be the least bit shy.

The incongruity intrigued him.

The elevator door opened, allowing a mother with two young children to enter. One of the children brushed up against the bag containing the angel, turning Phillip's thoughts to protecting his property and away from Grace. He switched hands and held the bag higher, watching the children with an eagle eye until the elevator reached the lobby, where everyone got out.

Once they arrived home, Phillip immediately drew the angel out of the bag so he could examine it more closely, without Grace watching him. Slowly, he ran his fingers over the flowing gown, analyzing the texture. He couldn't believe how stiff and coarse it now felt. He remembered how soft and pliable the angel had been when he tucked the balloons inside the arms. At that stage of reconstruction, Grace had washed all the original starch out and dried the angel, and the threads were in the same state as they would have been when Granny made the angel. The threads had not been pillowy soft, but they were delicate and smooth—very different than they were now.

"What are you doing with that thing? Can't you just put it down?"

Phillip grinned and lowered the angel to the coffee table. "Sorry. I can't help but think of what it looked like before we went through all that work to get it to stay like this." He pushed Neil's *TV Guide* aside and picked up a half-full cup of cold coffee left from the evening before. He then moved the angel into the center of the coffee table and walked toward the kitchen.

"This time, I'm making sure no more accidents happen," he called over his shoulder as he dumped the coffee sludge down the sink. "Either we got lucky with that coffee stain not setting, or God doesn't want anything to happen to that angel either."

"I dunno. Will you come back in here and give me a hand with this? We really don't have room for two couches, you know. Not that I want to give up either one. We've got to do something about this room. This isn't working."

Phillip sauntered back to the living room, but didn't enter. Instead, he leaned one hip against the door frame, crossed his arms, and grinned at his friend. "Maybe we should get a smaller television, then."

"Har-dee-har," Neil grumbled. "Zip it and get over here. I think if we can move our couch against that wall, slide your granny's couch there, we can put the recliner in the corner, and we'll have more room. We just won't be able to lean back in the recliner anymore."

"Then what's the point of the recliner?"

"Never mind. We'll think of something later. For now, we need room to walk."

"That's right." Phillip glanced at the angel in the center of the coffee table as he walked past. "We don't want any more accidents."

It took them nearly an hour, but they managed to rearrange the living room satisfactorily to a more comfortable and less cluttered arrangement.

Phillip groaned and reached his arms over his head to stretch a kink out of his back, while Neil flopped down on his granny's ex-couch.

"This is great," Neil sighed. "I wish there was some way to thank your granny for this. I feel like we should give her something, but she's getting rid of stuff now and doesn't want any more junk. Plus she won't have a backyard anymore, so I can't even offer to cut the grass when summer comes."

Phillip lowered himself to the recliner that no longer reclined. "I know what you mean. Maybe we can take her out for supper or something, although she cooks better than any restaurant. And for some reason, she likes to have people over and cook for them. Me, I'd rather go out. I know I sure had a nice time today with you and Grace."

Neil nodded, then rose off the couch. "Same. Come here for a sec. I think when we moved the TV stand, we accidentally shifted the television. It's crooked."

Phillip chose not to comment as he helped wiggle Neil's thirty-seven-inch television into position.

Neil grunted and straightened, but one hand remained on the heavy unit. "How's it now? Is that better?"

Knowing how picky Neil was about the television, Phillip stepped back. "I think so. No, turn it a little to the right." Phillip waited while Neil wiggled the television over half an inch. "I think that's just about right," he said as he continued to step backward to get the right perspective. "Maybe you should push it a little farther back. I think—"

His words were cut off when the edge of the coffee table caught him sharply at the backs of his knees. Phillip flailed his arms as he stumbled backward. This time, instead of just bumping the table, he knocked it sharply with the backs of his legs, hard enough to knock the table askew from its perfect placement in its new place in the room.

"Youch," he grumbled as he leaned over to rub the back of his left knee. "That stings. Maybe we aren't going to have as much space as…" His voice trailed off as he glanced around the room, his attention stopping at the coffee table.

The empty coffee table…

"The angel!" he gasped as he looked down to the floor.

The angel lay on the ground beside him.

Flattened.

Neil ran to his side. "No!" he exclaimed. "Is it bad?"

Phillip picked the angel up. Together they stared at the clear imprint of Phillip's shoe, accompanied by a black smudge across the middle of the gown.

With a shaking hand, Phillip managed to brush off a few grains of dirt until the black mark had been reduced to a gray smudge. He tried to be both gentle and firm as he poked and prodded at the imprint, trying to raise the decorative bumps and patterns of the squashed section so the shape of his shoe couldn't be seen. But, no matter how hard he tried, the visible mark of his shoe, especially the heel, still remained, nor could he press out the sharp folds on each side of the gown.

The complicated procedure for washing and restarching the angel ran through his mind.

Phillip cringed and squeezed his eyes shut.

When he opened them, he saw Neil staring at him.

Neil grinned weakly. "At least you already got rid of

the coffee cup from the table, so it's not as bad as before. What are you going to do?"

Phillip made one last attempt to brush off the gray mark. Failing that, he poked again at the distinct folds on either side of the angel's gown. When that didn't make a difference either, he sighed and turned his head to stare at the phone. "I think I need to call Grace."

Chapter 5

Grace had barely walked in the door after a hard day of work at the bank when the phone rang.

"Hey, Grace, it's me, Phil."

Grace felt herself break out into a wide smile, despite the fact that she was alone, except for her cat, who still hadn't moved to greet her even though she'd been gone all day.

"Hi, Phil. How are you?"

Instead of a reply, a silence hung over the phone for a few seconds.

He cleared his throat. "Not all that great, actually. I don't know how to say this, but I had a little accident with the angel last night. I kind of squished it. I'm sorry, but I need your help again."

Her smile dropped, and her heart sank, as the picture of all the work involved in washing, starching, and reshaping the angel flashed through her mind. "Oh," she mumbled.

Phil's voice dropped about an octave. "Can I come over?"

"I guess we don't have much choice."

"I haven't had dinner yet; have you?"

Grace glanced up at the clock on the stove. "No. I just got home from work. I had to stay late."

"Tell you what. I'll pick something up on the way there. It's the least I can do. Burger and fries okay?"

"Uh, sure," she mumbled. "I'll see you in fifteen minutes."

They mumbled quick goodbyes, and Grace hung up.

The fifteen minutes gave her just enough time to quickly straighten the kitchen, bring out the starch and spool of wire, and put on a pot of coffee pending Phil and Neil's arrival.

When the buzzer sounded to open the main door, she was ready if not psyched up for the job ahead. From habit, she stepped into the hall to wait for the elevator door to open and her guests to arrive. However, when the door slid open, only one guest stepped out.

"Phil? Where's Neil?"

He shrugged his shoulders. "I don't know. Maybe he had to work overtime, too. He wasn't home yet by the time I called you. I didn't want to wait because now I know from experience how long the whole thing takes, so I came alone. I hope that's okay. Besides, this time it is entirely my fault that the angel got hurt, so I figure I should be the one to fix it."

Grace felt a grin tugging the corners of her mouth. "'Hurt'?"

Phil's blush was most endearing. "It's not wrecked. Unlike last time, I know it's fixable. It's not exactly broken, so that wasn't the right word either. I stepped on it, and I figured that's gotta hurt, so..."

Grace giggled and led Phil inside her apartment. "To think you were teasing me the other day about personifying her. You're just as bad."

"I'm not personifying *it,*" he said, emphasizing the gender-neutral word. "But if I did, I would say *he* when talking about it."

Grace shook her head as Phil followed her into the kitchen and to the table in the center of the room. "He. She. It. You're addling my brain. Why don't we just call her Angelica and get rid of the pronouns. Besides, I feel like I should know her by now. She should have a real name."

Phil laid the angel a safe distance away on the edge of the kitchen table and began emptying the hamburgers and fries from the second bag. "I said before that angels were always seen as men. How about calling *him* Michael?"

"Michael. Well, that certainly shows imagination." Grace let her sentence hang, but Phil apparently missed her sarcasm.

She sighed. "Can't you think of something a little more original?"

Phil grinned as he pushed one hamburger and an envelope of fries across the table toward her. "If we're going to go through with this, how about something appropriate for either male or female. You know, like…uh…" He paused for a few seconds, drumming his fingers on the table. "Snicklefritz."

"Snickle…I thought you were serious."

Phil raised one palm in the air. "Hold on. Let's not argue. Let's say thanks for our food and eat. This stuff is bad enough while it's warm, but it will be really bad when it's cold. We can decide on a name while we eat."

"Of course. You're right," Grace said as she bowed her head.

Phil paused for a moment, then cleared his throat. "Thank you, Lord, for so many things. First for the food before us and the way you take care of all our needs. Thank you also for friends to share these things with and for friends we can go to when we need help. Please bless our time together, that we will be productive and successful. Amen."

"Amen," Grace mumbled as all her present thoughts deserted her. As soon as Phil had finished speaking, Grace had planned to give him a list of gender-neutral names that currently only were used for females but had been male in the past. However, at his heartfelt prayer, all thoughts of taking him on in a battle of one-upmanship deserted her.

Twice he'd referred to her as a friend. He hadn't been carefully nondescript the way people prayed during a meal at a banquet or celebration where the group was composed of fellow believers who weren't necessarily friends. Phil hadn't even remotely hinted that she was an acquaintance or merely the girlfriend of a friend, but his own friend.

The first time he'd come to her, they hadn't known each other well. Now, less than a week after spending actual time together, things had somehow changed. She'd already told herself that it was only natural she would like Phil, being Neil's best friend. Now it struck her that she felt differently about Phil than she did Neil's other friends. With Phil she felt an instant kinship, although she couldn't put her finger on why.

"Okay, I take back Snicklefritz. If we're going to be serious about picking a name for him-slash-her, then how about Terry or Gerry or something like that?"

Trying to look thoughtful, Grace swirled a fry in her blob of ketchup. "That depends if you spell those names with an *i* or a *y*."

"Grace, we're not going to be writing the angel a letter or filling out a legal document. We're only picking a name to get over this gender problem we seem to be having. If you can't come up with any good ideas, then it's up to me."

Grace thought that picking up the angel would have helped her look studious, but unfortunately, she couldn't take the chance of getting any fry-grease from her fingers on the angel. "Well, since last week we needed to remove that coffee splotch, and today we need to remove some kind of dirt from your shoes, I thought we could name him-slash-her Spot."

Phil's eyes widened, and Grace's breath caught. She couldn't stop watching his face as his lips quivered, growing into a full smile. As his smile grew, laugh lines appeared at the corners of his eyes, and he broke out into a hearty laugh. When he finally quieted, he swiped at his eyes with the corner of his napkin. "That was pretty good and unfortunately appropriate. But I don't think I'd want to explain that one if Granny ever heard us calling him Spot. Got any other suggestions?"

"The angel is not a him. Look at her, Phil. She's wearing a long flowing gown, and she's got long blond hair. That angel is a woman."

"Back in Bible days, the men wore long flowing things. I forget what they were called. They also had long hair. Although, I don't think people living in that area of the world had blond hair."

"I give up. My *Name Your Baby* book is in my bedroom. I'll go get it and pick a nice, gender-neutral name for you."

Phil smirked. "You're reading a *Name Your Baby* book? Why?"

Suddenly, before Grace could reply, his grin faded, and his face paled. He lowered his head and picked up the empty envelope for his fries, staring at it intently as he spoke, never once raising his eyes to her. "I'm sorry. I shouldn't have asked. It's none of my business. Before you got me all distracted, I believe I was going to ask you if you thought it was possible to get the angel finished tonight, since we've done it before and now we know what we're doing."

All Grace could do was stare at Phil. She hadn't thought of the implications of admitting she owned such a book, but she could well imagine what he thought, especially since her admission that it was in her bedroom probably indicated she was currently reading it, which she wasn't.

"Don't be embarrassed, Phil. It's not what you might think. This is a one-bedroom apartment. I don't know why it was designed this way, but the bedroom is huge. It's so big I put my bookcase in there instead of in the living room. I have a lot of books; I just can't seem to give them away. I guess I'm just cheap. My sister gave me her *Name Your Baby* book after she had her two kids, she told me 'just in case' I'll ever need it." Grace made a halfhearted laugh. "My sister isn't very subtle. I'm not reading it now. I have no reason to. But the book is in my bookcase for possible future use. Feel better?"

He raised his head, and Grace was pleased to see the color returning to his face, plus a little extra pink in his cheeks. "Yeah. Sorry. You didn't have to explain."

Grace smiled. "I know that. I just wanted to. Excuse me. I'll be right back."

Within a minute she had found the book and had returned to her seat at the kitchen table. While she was gone, she noted that Phil had made himself at home and poured them two cups of coffee.

Not wanting to take too much time, Grace flipped through the book, skimming as quickly as she could to find appropriate gender-neutral names. However, every time she mentioned a name, Phil didn't like it.

After he rejected a dozen allegedly unsuitable names for various reasons, Grace snapped the book shut and smacked it down onto the tabletop. "I thought we were going to pick something quick, then get down to business, which is seeing what we can do about fixing up the angel again. I haven't even really looked at the damage yet."

Phil rested his elbows on the table, cupped his chin in his palms, and grinned. "I dunno. This is kinda fun. Did you know my cousin Trevor and his wife Janice are expecting a baby in the spring? I wonder if this is what it's like when parents-to-be are picking out a name for their baby."

Grace sputtered into her coffee. "I don't know."

"I know you teach Sunday school. You like kids, don't you? You said your sister gave you the book as a not-so-subtle kind of hint. That aside, do you think you'd like to have kids of your own someday? Not everybody does."

Grace nearly choked, even though she thought she'd worked the first coughing fit out of her system. She nearly asked him why he was asking her such things but stopped short. Phil wasn't even looking at her. He was staring off into space, lost in his own thoughts.

Grace cleared her throat. "I guess so. What about you?"

"Yeah. I would. I didn't really have much time to talk to Trev on the weekend when we were at Granny's, but I've been thinking about him a lot. I'm older than he is, but Trevor was the first of the guys in the family to get married, and now he and Janice are soon going to hear the pitter-patter of little feet. He seems really happy and excited about it, and he's making me wonder what it would be like. I've been thinking for awhile now that I wouldn't mind settling down and having a family and all that. When God puts the right woman in my path, of course."

Grace didn't reply, and Phil didn't say any more. He only continued to stare unseeingly at a blank spot on the wall behind her.

Instead of picking up the book, Grace watched Phil.

She hadn't realized that men thought about getting married and settling down until a relationship struck them in the head. Apparently, she was wrong. As far as she knew, and according to Neil, Phil wasn't currently seeing anyone, yet he was obviously thinking about marriage fitting into his future.

He didn't seem to notice or care that no one was talking, so Grace took advantage of the silence to study him.

Even though he wasn't classically handsome, Phillip McLean was by no means ugly. With his medium brown hair and average height, as well as his usually quiet nature, he tended to blend into a crowd. Perhaps that was why Grace had never taken notice of him before. But more than his appearance, Grace was learning that he had a kind heart and a noble character, as well as a pleasant sense of humor. Again, she reminded herself that it was only natural she would like him, being Neil's friend. She had no doubt that he would make some woman a fine husband one day, and one day fairly soon, if he really was as ready to settle down as he said he was.

Phil's goofy little half smile straightened, he blinked a few times, and returned his attention to her. "I'm sorry, Grace. I shouldn't let myself get so distracted. What was that name you suggested? Dale, right? I think that's fine. Let's hereby christen Granny's angel *Dale* and get on with it."

"Yes, Dale is a good name. Let's go wash our hands, and we can get to work on fixing Dale."

Grace took the first turn to wash her hands. While she waited for Phil to finish in the bathroom, she picked up the angel and examined it. First she brushed at the offending gray smudge with her fingertips, knowing full well that Phil had already done his best to wipe it off.

As expected, it didn't come off, but that didn't mean it wouldn't with a little persuasion. After all, if it was from Phil's shoe, it was dry dirt and therefore had not soaked into the fibers of the angel like the coffee.

Phil appeared behind her to watch over her shoulder.

Grace picked at the dirt with her fingernail. To her satisfaction, some of the offending dirt actually came off.

"This is encouraging," she mumbled as she continued to

pick at it. When only a small speck remained, she handed Dale to Phil. "I'll be right back."

Using the damp corner of a clean tea towel, Grace managed to remove all of the mark.

"Wow! That's great!" Phil exclaimed over her shoulder. "We didn't have to wash Dale again. But what about the folds?"

Grace poked at the fold lines. "They're not that bad. I have an idea." Again, she handed the angel to Phil while she removed her plant mister from beneath the kitchen sink. Using a minimal amount of water, she sprayed only the lines of the fold. Being very gentle so she didn't stretch the shape out, Grace prodded the lines out, pressing the gown back into the correct shape.

Again, she handed the angel back to Phil.

"This is great, but I remember last time the dampness spread and the whole thing went soggy on me."

"That's not going to happen because this time nothing's really wet except for those two thin lines. Also, this time there's no soap or detergent involved, only water. Wait here. I'll be right back."

Grace returned with her blow-dryer and set to work. In only a few minutes, the wet spots were perfectly dry, and Dale was back to normal.

For the last time, she handed the angel back to Phil.

"Wow," he muttered as he ran his fingers over it. "I can't even tell anything was wrong. I don't know what to say."

"Don't worry about it. Since we're done, how would you like to go into the living room and finish our coffee there?"

"That would be great."

Grace topped off the mugs, and they carried them into the living room. Grace stifled her smile when she noted that, in addition to the mug, Phil also took the angel with him instead of leaving her on the kitchen table.

Once in the living room, Phil immediately headed for

her recliner. He placed the mug on the magazine stand beside the recliner but kept the angel in his lap. Without saying a word, he leaned back fully in the chair. With the angel lying on top of his stomach, Phil raised his arms to rest his hands behind his head, linked his fingers, and sighed. "I can't help myself. We had to rearrange the living room, and our recliner no longer reclines. I have to enjoy this while I can."

Grace smiled with her lips pressed to the rim of her coffee mug, but as soon as she sipped the warm liquid, her smile turned to a grimace. "Yuk!" Grace moved the mug away from her face, stuck out her tongue, and then wiped her mouth on her sleeve. "I think I have your coffee. This has a ton of sugar in it."

She leaned forward and put the mug down on the coffee table to allow herself to stand up and trade mugs with him, but before she could raise herself, Phil hopped out of the recliner. He set the angel in the middle of the recliner and was in front of her with her errant mug in seconds flat. "Sorry," he said as they traded mugs.

"How can you drink that? How much sugar do you have in there?"

"Only two spoons."

Grace shook her head at the thought of ingesting so much sugar in one cup. "That was awful. I don't use any sugar in my coffee."

"I guess you're sweeter than I am. I really need all that sugar."

Mug in hand, Phil returned to the recliner, but he didn't sit down. "Hey! Your cat has made himself at home on the recliner, right next to Dale."

Grace grinned. "Usually Tiger claims that chair as his own. I'm surprised he wasn't there in the first place, before you got there. But now that you've made it nice and warm, you've given him a reason to reclaim his territory and an open invitation to do so when you left the chair to come to me. I'm almost surprised he didn't hop up on your lap when you first sat in his chair. I guess he figures that Dale is better company than you are."

"Forget it, Cat," Phil grumbled as he set the coffee mug on the magazine stand. With both hands free, he picked up the angel with one hand and the cat with the other. "I got first dibs this time, and I'm bigger than you." Phil lowered Tiger to the floor and reestablished his place in the recliner, still keeping the angel firmly secure in his hand.

To Phil's obvious dismay, Tiger was not ready to give up his favorite spot. The second he had a chance, Tiger leapt into Phil's lap. Once there, and evidently confident he wasn't going to be pushed off, Tiger curled around the angel atop Phil's stomach and began to purr.

Phil craned his neck back and stared at the party in his lap. "It's pointless to argue with him, isn't it?"

"Yup."

"I don't care about my T-shirt, but is he going to get hair all over Dale?"

"Shouldn't, but even if he loses a few hairs, it's easy to pick them off. You've got to admit that it feels good to have him all cuddled up on top of you, doesn't it?"

Phil smiled as he stroked the fur behind Tiger's ears. With Phil's gentle ministrations, Tiger's purring grew louder. "I suppose," Phil mumbled. "I'm not much of a cat lover, but I don't mind this. He's not really much of a Tiger, is he?"

"No, he's not. I called him that because of his orange coloring, and he's got a few stripes."

They chatted comfortably until Grace noticed the time and realized that, since she had to be at work early the next morning, it was past her bedtime. They mutually agreed on how fast the evening had gone, and Grace saw Phil to the door.

She stepped out into the hall with him, but instead of walking toward the elevator, Phil turned around.

He lowered his head and stared at the angel in his hands. "Grace, you're wonderful. I know it ended up being easy to fix this time, but still, I didn't know what to do. I wouldn't have been able to do it without you. You saved my hide again. I had a really nice evening, too. Sorry to have overstayed my welcome on a work night. I owe you big time for this."

As he raised his head to look at her, Phil's glowing smile and the warmth in his gorgeous gray eyes did funny things to Grace's stomach.

Grace's breath caught in her throat. She had no right to be entranced with Phil's smile. She was dating his best friend. What was happening was wrong.

"It's okay," she mumbled. "You paid for my supper and hand-delivered it. That's payment enough."

"I disagree, but I'll deal with that another time. Good night, Grace."

Before she could respond, Phil turned and walked down the hall to the elevator.

Rather than stand and watch him as he waited, the second he pushed the button, Grace shuffled backward into her apartment and closed the door behind her.

Fortunately, she wouldn't have to deal with seeing Phil until Sunday, nearly a week away.

And, fortunately, that would be when she was at church with Neil, where she was safe.

Chapter 6

"Honey, I'm ho-ome," Phillip called out as he walked in the door.

The drone of the hockey game accompanied Neil's reply. "I guess she fixed it, judging by how long you were there."

Phillip didn't want to mention that the angel only took minutes to fix. The other two hours he spent at Grace's, the two of them simply yakked. Instead, he merely held the angel out for Neil to see, even though he knew Neil wasn't really interested. "Yup."

"Looks good. Pass it! Pass it! Argh!"

Phillip sighed, knowing he wasn't going to get any good conversation out of Neil so close to the end of what was obviously a close game. "I think I'm going to go to bed. Catch you sometime tomorrow."

"Yeah, see ya. Hey! High-sticking! There better be a penalty coming! Whoa! He scores! All right! One more and we've got 'em! Less than a minute left! We can do it!"

Phillip didn't bother to comment. He placed the angel in the middle of the table. "Good night, Dale, Neil."

"Night," Neil mumbled, too engrossed in the replay of the last goal to notice the mention of another name besides his own.

Phillip crawled into bed but only ended up staring at the ceiling.

As clear as the replay of the last goal to Neil, everything Phillip had said to Grace repeated over and over in his head. He couldn't believe the things he'd admitted to her. He'd never talked about such things in his life, not even to Neil, his best friend. Not that men never thought about getting married, because he was sure other men did. He just wasn't sure they ever talked about it seriously between themselves. Whenever his usual group of single friends discussed marriage, it was always griping and half joking about the loss of personal freedom and being shouldered with financial responsibility and a nagging wife.

Phillip knew it wasn't so. Marriage was a partnership between two people who loved and needed each other. The time had come where Phillip wanted his life to have more meaning than simply going back and forth to work. More and more, Phillip felt an emptiness inside, and he wanted to fill the hole with a woman who could need him and be his partner in life. But so far, God had not answered his prayers.

As much as he wondered what it would be like to be married, he couldn't imagine it because he had no one to fill in the missing half of the equation. The best he could do was think of his cousin Trevor and his wife, Janice, who seemed to be very different, yet a perfect match. The bottom line was both were strong believers, which fortified a happy relationship.

Likewise, Grace and Neil were both strong believers, which made Phillip wonder if one day they would announce a pending engagement. So far Phillip hadn't seen them together often enough to imagine that happening. Yet, because Neil and Grace had been dating each other exclusively for the past year, Phillip had to consider one day such an announcement had to be a strong possibility.

As to his own future wife, Phillip had no idea what kind of woman she would be, other than someone who shared his faith and someone who liked the great outdoors. He wasn't asking God for the perfect wife, just one who would be perfect for him. Again, his words to Grace, that he was waiting for God to put the right woman in his path, echoed in his head.

If he'd said the same thing to anyone else, Phillip wouldn't have been surprised if, over the next month, he was suddenly swarmed with marriage-hungry women. With Grace, he knew his words would go no further. He'd never said so openly what was on his heart, yet with Grace, it came naturally.

He still couldn't figure out what it was Neil had been referring to when Neil had referred to Grace as shy. Although Phillip wouldn't have exactly called her talkative, conversation between them never lagged. He hadn't known Grace long, but Phillip found Grace quite responsive to his comments and queries. In the few times there had been silences between them, it was never uncomfortable or strained. One thing he had noticed about Grace was that she tended to think everything through to the last possible conclusion before commenting. That didn't make her shy. It simply made her thoughtful and a bit on the quiet side, and there was nothing wrong with that.

In fact, rather than being bad, Phillip appreciated her tendency to think before she spoke. When someone took more time to think things through, that usually meant a person was less likely to jump to conclusions and more likely to weigh a situation fairly and of its own merit.

Phillip knew he sometimes tended to react too quickly, and because of that, he often found himself in trouble. Because he knew he tended to be decisive and a bit aggressive, he'd never really developed a friendship with anyone whom he would call shy, as shy people tended to back away from him.

Phillip rolled over and pulled the blanket up to his chin. Not only was Grace not backing away from him, he found her easy to talk to. And, once he really talked to her, he'd discovered a playful sense of humor that caught him completely by surprise. He couldn't remember the last time he'd laughed so hard as when Grace made her silly little comment about naming the angel Spot.

With that in mind, Phillip saw great potential in Grace. Neil may have considered her shy, but Phillip didn't think it would take much prodding to make her un-shy and really shine in a crowd.

As sleep finally started to take him, Phillip grinned and pressed his face into his pillow. The next time he saw Grace would be on Sunday, in church, where it was crowded.

And he could hardly wait.

"Come on up, Phil."

At the buzz, Phillip pulled the apartment-building door open and headed through the lobby for the elevator. Like every other time, by the time the elevator door opened on Grace's floor, she was waiting for him in the hall.

"How did it go last night?" he asked as he followed her inside and closed the door behind him.

"Great! Thank you so much for letting me borrow Dale for the day. I didn't expect your granny to come, what with her moving in a couple of weeks, but she was there. She said she came to Craft Night because she needed the break from looking at all those boxes. She also said she wanted to give away some of her craft supplies to people who would use and appreciate them. You should see all the knitting needles she gave me. Your granny is so nice. Did you know your granny made Dale when she was only twenty years old? She was really pleased that you let me borrow Dale to show all the ladies. I think that was the encouragement many of them needed to try to learn to crochet. Of course, I didn't tell your granny about the name, I just called *her*—" Grace emphasized the female pronoun "—your Christmas angel. We can keep the name Dale as our little secret."

Phillip didn't care about the ladies' craft group passing the angel around to check out how such things were made. But, the thought of his granny looking closely at Dale made him feel faint.

He lowered himself into the kitchen chair and picked Dale up from the middle of Grace's table. "Did she say anything?" he asked as he turned the angel over, trying to remember if anything had been changed from the way Granny had shaped the angel before the washing and reshaping fiasco.

"She did seem a little surprised at how nicely Dale had stayed so bright over the years. I suggested that maybe Dale just seemed brighter because of the new natural-light fluorescent bulbs. You know the room we use for our craft meetings. It's the one the preschool uses during the daytime. Since it's in the basement and there aren't any windows, Pastor suggested the special full-spectrum lighting at the last general meeting. It turned out to be a wise choice."

"Yeah," he mumbled as he set the angel down, much more interested in Thursday evening's craft meeting than the decisions made by the church's budget committee last spring. "Did she say anything else?"

"No, she didn't. We must have done a good job in positioning the arms and wings in the shape and position they were in before, because after commenting on the whiteness, she got right into showing everyone basic crocheting, and then gave the more experienced crocheters some wonderful tips."

Phillip felt himself sag with the relief of knowing their efforts had been successful. If Granny hadn't noticed a change in front of the other ladies, she certainly wouldn't notice Christmas morning amidst all the activity, when the focus was on the family, not the ornaments.

He started to lean back into the chair, but all movement stopped when he looked at Grace, who was now also sitting. Leaning slightly forward, her elbows rested on the table. She cupped her chin in her palms, and she was looking straight at him with a dreamy smile that froze him on the spot.

"I know how you feel," she said with an airy sigh. "I was so nervous that she was going to ask me if something was wrong, but so many people complimented her on Dale, she forgot all about the nice white color. She tried to tell everyone that making such a thing wasn't as hard as it looked. Of course I know better. Making a crocheted tree topper is definitely as hard as it looks."

Phillip cleared his throat. "Don't ask me. All I know is that *he*—" Phillip emphasized the male pronoun "—looks great on top of the Christmas tree every year."

Suddenly, Grace jumped to her feet. "I'm sorry! I made coffee in case you wanted some, but, then again, you probably have better things to do with yourself than sit here with me on a Friday night."

Phillip shrugged his shoulders. "Not really. I didn't have any plans. As you know, Neil had to go do something with his parents, so he won't be home until late. It's started snowing again, so I was just going to go home and shovel the driveway, watch a bit of television, and go to bed. Having coffee with you is much more fun than shoveling snow."

"Flatterer."

Phillip grinned as he rose and walked to join Grace at the coffeepot on the counter, not wanting her to serve him. "Yeah, that's me. Mr. Charm. Tall, dark, and handsome, too."

"Oh, puh-leeze."

He stood to the side as she filled both mugs. "Seriously, though, I have to admit I was pretty nervous when Granny phoned me Thursday morning to ask if the craft ladies could borrow Dale for the night. It's a good thing we got *him* all fixed in time."

Grace nodded, then grimaced as she made a big show out of dumping two spoonfuls of sugar into Phillip's coffee mug. "I know. We'd planned to have Mrs. Capstan show the group how to make a Thanksgiving centerpiece, but something else came up at the last minute. The monthly Thursday night craft meetings are a ministry to the neighborhood ladies, as well as for our own church members. Your granny was so sweet to come up with such a charming idea on short notice. You should have seen her up at the front, demonstrating."

Phillip stepped away from Grace to get the cream out of her fridge. When he turned back to face her, he froze. All he could do was stare as Grace grinned from ear to ear while describing his granny's impromptu demonstration.

Twice in one day, Grace's adorable smile left him feeling like he'd just been poleaxed.

He wished he could make her smile like that. Phillip wondered if he could find out from Neil other things that made Grace smile. He also wondered if Neil was as enamored with Grace's smile as he was.

At the thought, the cream carton nearly fell from his hand. Of course he liked her—Grace was his best friend's girlfriend, and it was only to be expected that he'd like her to some degree. Since both of them shared a relationship with Neil, it seemed natural that they could be friends, too.

Phillip shook his head to get his thoughts back to where they should have been in the first place. As Grace continued to expound on his granny's performance, she snickered while she made some kind of hand motions to imitate what his granny had done in front of the roomful of women.

Finally starting to pay attention to what she was saying rather than how she said it, Phillip listened to the tail end of Grace's description of his granny in action.

He cleared his throat. "Speaking of finishing up making stuff like that, I've always wondered about the hair." He added cream to both coffee mugs and returned the cream container to the fridge, thankfully without incident. But instead of picking up his mug, he picked up the angel. "The hair has fascinated me since I was a kid. Look at it." To emphasize his point, Phillip ran his fingers through the angel's golden locks. "It looks so real. I wonder what it's made of."

Grace took one sip of coffee from her mug, rested it on the counter beside Phillip's mug, and reached over to remove the angel from his hands. "Way back in the olden days, they did actually use real hair for stuff like this."

Phillip couldn't hold back a shudder. "Gross," he muttered as he released the angel to her.

"Don't worry. This is synthetic hair. It's not very good in comparison to what they use now, but it's the same thing they used for doll hair around the late forties, which is when she would have made this. See?"

Grace moved her free hand toward the angel's head, but before she actually touched the hair, her movement stopped. Abruptly, she picked off a number of cat hairs from the wings.

"I'm so sorry, Phil. Because she's so pretty, I put Dale

on display on the coffee table while I was at work. When I got home, I found Tiger on the coffee table, too, curled around her. I don't know why Tiger has taken such a liking to something like this. Part of me wants to make one for Tiger, since he likes it so much, but I'm certainly not going to go through all that work just so it can be used as a cat toy."

After she picked off the last of the offending cat hairs, Grace slid her fingers into the angel's fine hair and separated it at the roots. "On plastic dolls, the hair comes through holes in the doll's head, but in this case, your granny pulled the hair through a porous fabric, which she clipped and sewed to make round, then stitched it onto Dale's head, almost like a mini wig. See?"

"I can't see anything."

She stepped closer and pushed the hair flatter. "There. See how it's done?"

"Yeah. I see how it's made now." Phillip looked up, about to comment that to make the hairpiece alone must have taken hours. Before he could speak, his breath caught in his throat. In order to show him how the hair was attached, Grace stood so close, he could see the variances of browns in her eyes.

More than her eyes, while standing so close together, his attention fixated on her lips. Soft, full lips.

Kissable lips.

Almost as if the thought delivered a physical blow, Phillip stumbled back a step.

"Phil?"

His stomach churned as what he had been thinking rolled over in his head.

He had wanted to kiss Grace. He still wanted to kiss her. And that was wrong.

In order to refocus his thoughts, he tore his attention from her lips and concentrated on her eyes. Her beautiful, big, brown eyes. Limpid, thoughtful eyes. Eyes that shone with a gentle sweetness he'd never noticed before.

Phil shook his head. "You know, I think I must be more tired than I thought."

Grace's eyebrows knotted. "Are you okay, Phil? You are kind of flushed all of a sudden."

Before he realized what she was about to do, she pressed her palm to his forehead.

Phillip backed up so quickly, he bumped into the table. With the movement, her hand dropped from his forehead, but his skin seemed to burn from her touch. "What are you doing?" he choked out.

"Just checking to see if you've got a bit of a fever. You don't seem warm to me, but your face is a bit red."

Phillip suddenly felt strange. He didn't know if he was hot or cold, but suddenly the thought of shoveling the driveway held a lot of appeal.

"Sorry about the coffee, Grace. I think I should go. If I don't tackle that driveway tonight, it's going to be a killer to do in the morning."

"The driveway? But…" Her voice trailed off as she looked over his shoulder at the window and the snow falling outside. She cleared her throat. "That's okay. If you're going to shovel snow, you might need something to keep you warm. Let me loan you a travel mug for the coffee, and you can take it home."

Phillip didn't really want to borrow her mug, but he figured he would be out of there faster if he just accepted her offer rather than take the time to argue with her.

At the door, he mumbled a quick thank-you, then waited politely while she, in turn, thanked him for loaning Dale to her for the previous night. She didn't mention anything about Saturday, which was just as well for Phillip. He didn't know if Neil had made plans with Grace, but just in case Neil hadn't, Phillip didn't want to hear that Grace would be home alone on Saturday night. He needed time to sort his wayward thoughts, so seeing her Sunday in church as originally planned would be soon enough.

With a mug of coffee in one hand and the angel in the other, Phillip made his way to his car.

Despite the blustery conditions, Phillip enjoyed the drive home. He liked the snow. Today, the snow served as a reminder that in less than a week it would be Thanksgiving, and following that, the advent of the Christmas season and everything that went with it.

One thing that went with Christmas was winter, and winter meant shoveling snow.

By the time Phillip arrived at home, the snow was ankle-deep on the driveway that Neil had shoveled only a few days ago. He tromped up to the front door but, instead of going inside, Phillip turned around to enjoy the sights of the snow falling in his neighborhood.

The glow of the streetlights on the fresh falling snow lit the entire neighborhood, making everything clean and fresh as the new snow covered the old layer, which had become dirty since the last snowfall. White ribbons covered the tree branches, and all the houses were layered with white. Even the street was covered, the only thing marring the surface being Phillip's own tire tracks, and soon they would be covered, too.

Tomorrow, most of the driveways would be shoveled bare, and many yards would be decorated with lopsided snowmen fashioned by screeching children. For now, though, everything was smooth and fresh and quiet. The only sounds were the echoes of traffic in the distance, and Ralphie, his neighbor's dog, barking as he jumped around in the snow.

Phillip smiled as he sipped the coffee, remembering standing outside in such weather as a child, catching snowflakes on his tongue. Watching Ralphie running in circles, he wondered if dogs ever caught snowflakes on their tongues.

Almost in answer to his question, Ralphie became aware of Phillip standing in the yard and watching him. The energetic mutt lost interest in whatever he was doing and stood still, watching Phillip.

"Here, Ralphie, old boy," Phillip muttered. Because he still had the coffee mug in one hand, Phillip tucked Dale under his arm. Then, with his free hand, he patted his thigh to encourage the dog.

Clumps of snow flew in all directions as Ralphie bounded toward him. Today, probably because of the excitement of the new snow, Ralphie didn't sit in front of him when called. The dog jumped up toward Phillip's face.

"Down, boy!" Phillip laughed as he spoke.

To Phillip's surprise, Ralphie really did stop jumping. The dog stepped closer. Puffs of steam suspended in the air as Ralphie sniffed him.

Without notice, Ralphie emitted a low growl and lunged. Caught completely off guard by Ralphie's unusual response, Phillip remained still. Ralphie thrust his face under Phillip's arm. Before Phillip knew what had happened, Ralphie grabbed the angel in his mouth, turned, and ran.

Grace's comment about how Tiger had taken a liking to the angel and how Tiger had been sleeping with it all day echoed in Phillip's head.

Phillip dropped his keys and the coffee mug on the ground. "Ralphie! No!" he called out as he ran after the dog. Fortunately, Ralphie ran into his neighbor's backyard and straight into his doghouse.

Just as Phillip reached him, Ralphie lowered his head and shook the angel as if he were killing a rodent.

Not caring about his own safety while cornering a dog, Phillip stepped in front of the doghouse opening, blocking

Ralphie's path to escape. "Drop it!" he said, trying to keep his voice from trembling. He reached out one hand, not really expecting Ralphie to obey, which Ralphie didn't. Since Ralphie didn't run or growl, Phillip grabbed the angel with both hands and struggled to pry it out of Ralphie's mouth.

When he finally got it loose, Ralphie lunged again, but this time, Phillip was ready. He blocked the dog with his free hand and with his other thrust Dale under his jacket.

With his prey out of sight, Ralphie snuffled, then walked to his master's back door, sat, and barked to be let inside.

Phillip's feet wouldn't move. Still standing in his neighbor's backyard, he forced himself to sum up the damage.

Without looking at it, he knew he would have to rewash and restart the angel to eradicate the dog's saliva.

His heart sank when he looked at the right wing. An inch from the tip was a hole the size of Ralphie's tooth.

"No…" he muttered aloud as he pressed at the hole with a shaking finger.

The neighbor's patio door swooshed open and shut, leaving Phillip all alone in his neighbor's backyard.

Phillip closed his eyes and raised his face to the dark sky. The cold of the snowflakes landing and melting on his skin did nothing to refresh his troubled spirit.

He couldn't go back today, but he knew where he was going tomorrow.

Chapter 7

"It's not that bad, Phil. Really."

Grace raised her head just in time to see Phil running his fingers through his hair.

He rammed his hands in his pockets. "There's a hole in the wing, it's covered in dog drool, and it's all squished up. How can that not be bad?"

She held out the angel toward him. "It's not really a hole. No threads are broken; it's just a bit stretched. All I have to do is use a crochet hook and even out the stitches again, and then wash it and restarch it, which we've done once already. The second time we fix it up is bound to be easier than the first time, now that we know what we're doing."

Grace forced herself to smile at Phil in an attempt to ease his obvious distress. The procedure had taken them hours the first time, and then there were three of them working. Today Phil had come alone. Her only consolation was that she had saved the wire pieces, which were already cut and molded into the right shapes.

"Take heart. You know that old expression—troubles come in threes. This is three, so from here, everything will be fine."

He mumbled something she wasn't sure she wanted to hear.

"Come on, Phil, don't be that way. Dale is going to be fine."

"I suppose I should have seen this coming," she said over her shoulder as she walked into her bedroom to get her sewing kit while Phil waited in the hall. "The first time Dale got hurt was Neil's fault, the second time you did it. Now this time I'm afraid it's my fault, because that dog would never have attacked Dale if Tiger hadn't got his scent all over her."

Sewing kit in hand, she headed for the kitchen. Once again, Phil trailed behind her. "It's not your fault, Grace. It was my fault. I was too slow when Ralphie jumped up. I should have reacted sooner. Dale was under my arm when Ralphie grabbed him. I can't believe I was so slow, but I was standing there with my head in the clouds, enjoying the snow."

Grace pretended to shiver as she sat and dug into the case for her stitch ripper. "Enjoying the snow? You've got to be kidding. It was cold last night when you left. It's still cold now, even though the sun is shining."

Very carefully, Grace pulled off the halo and slowly picked at the stitches that held the hair in place. The meticulous sewing that had taken her half an hour to do came out in under a minute. Likewise, she began taking out the fine, invisible seam she'd so carefully manipulated to fasten the silk lining to the bottom of the crocheted gown in a fraction of the time it had taken to put it in.

"That hair looks awful lying there like that. It looks like you scalped poor Dale, and now by taking out the white stuff, you're gutting him like a fish."

"Phil!"

"Seriously, you're doing such a good job. Have you ever scaled and cleaned a fish?"

"Eww. I think not!"

"Well, I've got a deal for you. We should go fishing sometime next summer. I'll show you how to gut a fish, and then I'll cook the fish for you over the open campfire. Or if that doesn't suit you, I'll clean and gut the fish, and you can cook it over the fire."

"I don't think so."

One corner of Phil's mouth quirked up, and little crinkles appeared at the corners of his eyes.

All Grace could do was stare at him with her mouth hanging open. In the process, she stabbed her finger with the stitch ripper.

"Then how about this? You catch a fish, Neil can clean and gut it, we'll take it home, and I'll barbecue it."

Ignoring the pinch in her finger, Grace returned her attention to the task at hand, which was not getting lost in Phillip McLean's smoky-green eyes. She focused only on pulling the silk lining away from the gown. "I don't think so," she mumbled, keeping her head down so she wouldn't have to look at him.

"Or we can go to the marketplace and buy a fish already filleted, say we caught and gutted it, and get Neil to cook it."

Grace smacked the lining and angel down on the table. "What are you talking about? You're distracting me!"

"Sorry," he said, although his mischievous grin told her otherwise.

"Now you can go wash Dale in the sink, and I'll cook the starch. While it cools, we can insert the balloons, although it will be harder to do than last time, because this time Dale is wet and the rubber won't slip in quite so smoothly."

Phil lost his grin, instantly becoming serious. "You're right. I really am sorry. Have I told you how much I appreciate this?"

Grace's mouth opened, but no sound came out. As Phil stared unwavering into her eyes, she felt the heat of a blush flaming her cheeks. Unable to withstand the intense eye contact without melting, Grace stared down at an imaginary spot on the table.

She nearly jumped to the ceiling when Phil's warm hand covered hers on top of the table.

"Grace? Why won't you look at me? I was teasing about the fish stuff. I just feel bad for imposing on you again."

"It's okay," she mumbled, still not able to look up at him. "You're not imposing. I really don't mind doing this. I did it the first time as a favor to Neil, but now it's becoming a challenge."

Phil's voice lowered in pitch, coming out as a low rumble. "Do you like a challenge, Grace?"

She couldn't help herself. She couldn't not look at him as she replied. "That depends, I suppose. Fixing Dale for the third time isn't as big a challenge as fixing her the first time."

"I meant a different kind of challenge. How would you and Neil like to come with me to the grand opening for the new Christian coffeehouse tonight? I know it's going to be crowded, but it will be really fun. There's going to be a couple of top-name Christian musicians, followed by a worship time and then a time of fellowship. People have been encouraged to bring their non-Christian friends, so it will also be a good time for ministry. I haven't asked Neil because I forgot it was today until I was on my way here, but I'm sure he'll go if you go. I don't want to go alone."

Grace tilted her head and narrowed her eyes slightly as she studied Phil. One eyebrow quirked as he waited for her reply.

For tonight, she and Neil had agreed that they would get together, but they'd made no definite plans. The idea that Phil would be tagging along or, rather, that they were tagging along with Phil held a lot of appeal. She enjoyed her time with Phil, yet a modicum of guilt had started to creep in after spending so much time alone with him over the last couple of weeks, when she hadn't spent much time, if any, with Neil.

This time, though, she had the perfect solution.

Grace smiled and nodded. "That sounds like fun. I'd love to go, and I'm sure Neil would, too. You shouldn't go to things like that alone, and you shouldn't go as the odd man out in a threesome either. I have a friend who would probably enjoy coming with us to even out the numbers. How does that sound?"

Phil returned her smile, but somehow, the smile didn't seem to reach his eyes. "A friend?"

She nodded again. This time, she reached over and laid her hand over the top of his. "You don't have to be shy, Phil. June is really nice."

"I don't do blind dates. Have I met her before? Does she go to our church?"

"No, but she is a Christian. We've been friends for years. Trust me; you'll like her. I'm not saying anything has to come of it in the long run. All I'm saying is that making it a foursome will even out the numbers."

"I guess. Sure. Why not?"

Grace tried not to visibly show her relief. She didn't normally like loud music, but she couldn't turn down a Saturday night outing in total Christian company with people her own age, especially with Phil present. Because of the way he made her laugh, she could imagine how much fun he could be in a crowd.

"Great. So what now?"

"One of us should phone Neil now and see if he wants to go. Maybe he has plans and didn't tell you."

Grace shook her head. "No, Neil's great. He always tells me a few days in advance if he wants to go somewhere special. It seems to me he was thinking of renting a movie tonight for lack of a better idea. Why don't you phone Neil, and I'll phone June?"

Like typical men, Phil and Neil's conversation lasted only as long as it took to ask the question if Neil had other plans, which he didn't. As soon as Phil hung up, Grace phoned June, but all she got was her friend's answering machine. Grace left a message and returned to the kitchen, where she found Phil seated at the table with Dale in his hands.

Grace joined him at the table and folded her hands in front of her. "We can still go if I can't get ahold of June; it just won't be as much fun. If we're going to get good seats, we should probably have an early supper."

They both turned in unison to check the clock on Grace's kitchen stove.

Phil's eyebrows raised, and he lowered his head to check his wristwatch. "I can't believe this. It's nearly three o'clock. Are we going to have time to do everything we need to do? I still have to go home and change."

"Maybe, but it's not likely. I'd rather err on the side of caution, so therefore I have an idea. Let's just wash Dale and let her dry, like we did last time. Besides, it will be easier to work the balloons inside the arms and head when she's not wet. Also, it will be easier for me to even out the stitches where that dog stretched the spot on the wing when the threads are dry and free of starch. We're really not in any rush. We can wash Dale now, and then you could come back tomorrow when she's dry, and we'll finish the job."

"Good idea." As he spoke, Phil stood and began to roll up his shirtsleeves. "Like I said earlier, I feel bad imposing on you so much. I'll wash Dale, because you're the one who's going to be starching him."

Grace grinned. "I'm also the one who's going to fix *her* wing."

Phil crossed his arms over his chest. "But I'm the one who will be putting the balloons in *his* arms."

"But I'm doing *her* head."

A telltale grin tweaked at one corner of his mouth. Grace could see Phil struggling to dampen it. "And I'll be bracing *his* wings when the starching is done."

Likewise, Grace's lower lip quivered, and she couldn't stop it. "And when *she* is dry, I have to sew *her* hair and *her* halo back on, as well as the lining of *her* gown." The giggles Grace tried so hard to subdue could no longer be controlled. Grace burst out laughing, as did Phil.

When all the laughter subdued, Grace wiped a tear from the corner of one eye. "This is ridiculous, you know."

"Yeah, I know. But that's okay. I know that in the end, you'll see I'm right."

"Don't bet on it, Mister. Now we'd better get busy. While you wash Dale, I'll try to untangle the hair."

"Good idea. Where's the detergent?"

"Under the sink."

Without another word, Phil obediently located the detergent, filled the kitchen sink with warm water, and dunked Dale to begin his task. As he gently washed the angel, instead of working the tangles out of the hair, Grace watched Phil.

She'd never seen a man with his hands in the kitchen sink. When she was a child, her father never washed dishes. The task had always been done by her mother, then shared with her brother and sister as she and her siblings became old enough to handle the responsibility. Whenever she cooked for Neil, she left what didn't go in the dishwasher in the sink to soak and finished everything herself later, before bed. In the entire year she'd been dating Neil, he had never once cooked her dinner—most of the time they went out. The few times she ate at his house, they'd ordered in so there were no dishes to do.

Keeping his hands immersed in, the sudsy water, Phil turned his head and spoke to her over his shoulder. "How do I tell when this is washed enough? I don't feel any slime or anything anymore, but since *he* is under water, it's kind of hard to tell."

Something strange happened in the pit of Grace's stomach. Phil wasn't doing anything unusual. If she didn't know any better, it would have looked like he was simply washing dishes.

She couldn't believe how masculine he looked doing such a domestic chore. His stance and carefree pose told her he was relaxed and comfortable with himself, no matter what he did.

"If you think you've gotten off all the dog drool, then you probably have. Just make sure you do a double rinse to get all the soap out."

"What about fabric softener? I always use fabric softener at home when I do laundry. It makes everything smell nice. I don't know if guys are supposed to admit that."

"No. Fabric softener impedes a fabric's ability to absorb water, so it's best not to use any because we need the starch to be absorbed as much as possible into the cotton threads."

"Then maybe I should use more fabric softener on my shirts in the summertime. Then I won't have to wear a jacket when it rains."

Grace opened her mouth, but no sound came out.

"Okay, then that means I'm done. What should I do now?"

Her voice came out much too mousy, but she couldn't find the strength to speak normally. "I'll set up my dry-

ing rack in the bathtub—that's what I did last time. I'll
be right back."

Before he could respond, Grace dashed off. With shaking hands, she unfolded the wire rack and extended it
across the tub. She didn't know when or why Phil had
started to affect her, but he had.

Since the main reason she'd begun seeing Phil was because of Neil, Grace couldn't help but compare the two
men.

She'd developed a comfortable relationship with Neil,
partly because she always knew what to expect with him.
When she and Neil disagreed on something, which didn't
happen often, they always respected each other's choices
and decisions. She never had to play guessing games with
Neil. When Neil was up, he was up, and when he was
down, he was very down, and she could deal with it.

Another thing that she liked so much about Neil was
that once something earned a place in Neil's heart, he pursued it with enthusiasm and determination, pouring himself into it, body, mind, and soul. Even if she didn't like
hockey as much as he did, Grace couldn't help but admire
the way he diligently pursued the game he loved. In the
end, Neil's love for the game was an extension of his per-
sonality. She wondered how one day she would fit into
Neil's level of dedication, as it had been nearly a year that
they'd been exclusively dating each other.

Then there was Phil.

She couldn't quite figure him out, not that she knew him
well. In the past year, during whatever contact she'd had
with him, nothing seemed to rattle him until his granny's
angel became damaged. She supposed his ensuing panic
was the main reason she found herself drawn to him. His
reaction seemed to be borne solely out of concern for his
granny—he didn't want her feelings to be hurt by seeing he
had allowed something she treasured to become damaged.

Grace found his guilt that he'd let his granny down when she trusted him so endearing, she couldn't get him out of her mind. The sweetness of his sentiment made her want to help him, regardless of other relationships involved.

Plus, Phil made her smile. Not that he was a stand-up comic by any stretch of the imagination, but Phil possessed a sense of humor and general easy nature that shone through in everything he did. She could well imagine Phil staring up into the falling snow and ignoring all around him, not caring if anyone was watching him or not. Yet at the same time, once he made up his mind, it was made up, and nothing seemed to change it. For someone else, the two traits might not mix, yet with Phil, they did.

The more she saw of Phil, the more he fascinated her. But was that right?

"I think I wrung out all the excess moisture, like you said, without squeezing too hard. Are you ready for me? If you're not, I'm here, anyway."

Grace squealed and jumped to her feet at Phil's unexpected appearance. "Yes. Just lay Dale down in the middle, and I'll straighten her out."

"Will he be dry by tomorrow? Should we do this after church or tackle the job in the evening? If you need time to fix the wing, then maybe—"

The ringing phone cut off Phil's sentence.

Grace checked her watch. "That's probably June calling me back."

"I'll let myself out, then. We all have to get ready for tonight. Should I pick June up at her house, or will she be meeting you here? I'll need the address."

Grace hurried to the phone as Phil walked to the door. "I don't know," she called out as the distance between them increased. "I'll phone you after I talk to June. See you later."

The door clicked shut at the same time Grace lifted the receiver from the cradle.

"Hi, Grace. I got your message. That sounds like fun, but I'm not sure I want to be paired up with a guy I've never met before."

"Phil said much the same thing. Don't worry; it will be fine."

"I don't know…" Her friend's voice trailed off. "What's he like?"

Grace let a silence hang over the phone while she thought of how to best summarize Phil. Since she'd already spent a good portion of the last hour thinking about him, saying something about him should have been easy, but it wasn't.

In order to think better, Grace closed her eyes. In her mind's eye, she pictured Phil with his warm smile and sparkling eyes, which she still couldn't give a color to. Something in those eyes captivated her the first time she'd been alone with him, and they still did. Therefore, she didn't want to discuss that with June.

Instead, she made a mental list of Phil's finer attributes. In doing so, she also had to admit that she wanted to spend more time with Phil and get to know those attributes even better.

Since Dale only needed a few hours of work, the time spent with Phil would soon revert to the way they were before. That meant she wouldn't see Phil very often except for church on Sunday, when he didn't always sit with them, and he never joined them for lunch afterward.

She had hoped, though, that Phil felt the same way about their budding friendship as she did. If so, hopefully he might spend more time with her and Neil on the nights they didn't have specific plans. However if, after their outing tonight, Phil and June actually did hit it off, it would be only natural for Phil to spend his spare time with June instead of her.

Something strange happened in Grace's stomach, making her think she must have suddenly become very hungry and not noticed before.

"Grace? Are you there?"

"Oh, sorry," she mumbled, then cleared her throat. "Phil is very nice."

"Nice? Well… Okay, but only because you wouldn't have asked in the first place unless you thought it would be fun. Where are we all meeting?"

"Parking might be tight, so why don't we pick you up on the way?"

When June spoke, Grace could hear the smile in June's voice. "Great. I'll see you later."

As they hung up, Grace suddenly realized that she really didn't want her friend to come. She mentally kicked herself for the unbidden thought, as such thinking wasn't fair. She was really going with Neil, not Phil. She had no claims over Phil and his social life and no real reason to want to be part of it.

Besides, it had been her idea to invite June in the first place. Therefore, as a foursome, they would have fun.

Chapter 8

The phone rang just as Phillip walked in the door. He agreed on a time with Grace, since they were going to pick her friend up on the way to the coffeehouse, and hung up quickly.

"Neil? Where are you?"

Neil's voice drifted from down the hall. "I'm shaving."

Phillip made his way to the bathroom, stood in the doorway, leaned one hip into the door frame, and crossed his arms.

"I've got to ask you something."

"Mmm," Neil muttered as he dragged the razor down one cream-covered cheek.

"The other day you said Grace was shy. I don't think she's shy. She jumped at the chance to come tonight. She even invited a friend on short notice. And she certainly holds up her end of a conversation. What makes you think she's shy?"

Neil ran the razor under the tap but didn't resume shaving. With one cheek still coated with shaving cream, he turned to Phillip. "I dunno. I guess because she's so quiet most of the time. Whenever I ask her what she wants to do, she usually picks something simple for just the two of us. I'm really surprised she wants to go to the grand opening. It's going to be busy and crowded and noisy. If she has a good time, maybe I'll ask her if she wants to go to the next hockey game with me."

Phillip chose to reserve judgment on that one. "Have you ever met her friend June?"

Neil resumed shaving. "Nope."

"Have you met many of her friends?"

Neil made a number of short, quick strokes beneath his nose, then stood. "Not really, come to think of it. But she goes out shopping and stuff with them all the time. Girl stuff, I guess."

Phillip almost asked if Grace had met many of Neil's other friends, but stopped short. He hardly ever saw the two of them together, and not only was he Neil's best friend, he lived with Neil. He would be the one out of Neil's friends to see the most of Grace.

"She doesn't see much of your friends either. That's weird," he muttered.

Neil splashed a handful of water on his cheeks, then wiped his face with a towel. "Not really. I told you, she's shy."

"Shy is one thing, but she's certainly not a social outcast."

"I'm done. If you want to shave, the bathroom's yours. What do you want to do for supper? Maybe we should just grab a couple of burgers on the way to Grace's place."

Phillip blinked at the abrupt change of subject, which told him the topic was not open for discussion.

"Whatever." He leaned toward the mirror and rubbed his fingertips over his chin. "I don't really need to, but maybe I will shave. I suppose I should be trying to make a good first impression."

"Can't hurt. After all, when was the last time you had a girlfriend?"

Before Phillip could respond, Neil turned and disappeared into his bedroom to change, which was just as well. Phillip didn't want to talk about his love life with Neil, although he supposed he deserved Neil's little barb after questioning Neil so much about Grace.

After they changed, they were ready to go. Since Neil's truck only sat three people, Phillip became the designated driver. As Neil suggested, they grabbed a quick burger mid-route and continued on. Grace was ready and waiting in the lobby when they arrived, and they were quickly on their way to pick up her friend.

Beyond the number of passengers in the car, Phillip hadn't thought in advance about the seating arrangements until they arrived at June's house. Both Neil and Grace scooted out of the front seat to sit in the back, offering the front seat to June.

All of a sudden, Phillip felt very "paired up."

Fortunately, June looked as nervous as he felt. The fact didn't help him to relax, although it did make him feel a bit better.

Grace managed to ease some of the initial discomfort by doing her best to keep conversation going. To Phillip's surprise, she did most of the talking, inserting comments and questions from the backseat almost nonstop, which he greatly appreciated. However, her actions once again contradicted Neil's statement that she was shy. Yet, Neil was the one dating her, and Neil allegedly knew her better.

Once they gained admission and purchased four flavored lattes, they were seated at a table. Now that Phillip wasn't driving, it was time to work through the initial awkward stage of a blind date. During the trip to the coffeehouse, he had made up his mind that no matter what happened, he would make the best of the situation. June wasn't a complete stranger—she was Grace's friend—and so being, they had at least one thing in common. That gave him someplace to start.

He pushed his mug to the side, rested one elbow on the table, leaned his chin on his knuckles, turned to June, and smiled politely. "I've never seen you here before. Do you come here often?"

Out of the corner of his eye, he saw Grace smile for just a split second. June didn't smile at all. She blinked a couple of times, then silently stared at him with wide eyes.

Since the lights hadn't yet been turned down for the featured guest musician, every nuance of June's face showed quite clearly.

He couldn't help but compare the two women.

Grace's face was round and cute, and her big brown eyes accented her inward sweetness. In contrast, June's face was more pixielike in appearance. Thin and fine featured with a slightly pointy chin, she could have been called delicate if she weren't nearly as tall as he was. Her short, blond hair would have given any other woman a boyish appearance, except that June was so lovely, no one could ever call her unfeminine.

If he had to judge her on appearance alone, he would have to say that June was prettier than Grace, yet he found Grace more attractive. However, he knew he had to be fair to June. Technically, he wasn't there with Grace, he was there with June, and he shouldn't have been thinking about Grace.

Yet he was. He couldn't help it.

Phillip cleared his throat, straightened in the chair, and clasped his hands in front of him on the table. "Okay, that didn't work. I'll try again. What's a nice girl like you doing in a place like this?"

June didn't respond, but Phillip could see Grace nibbling on her bottom lip, trying to hold back a grin, which gave him the encouragement he needed.

He put on his best puppy-dog face, blinked a few times, quirked one eyebrow, and then leaned forward toward June. "If I followed you home, would you keep me?"

June's mouth dropped open. Grace groaned from across the table. Beside her, Neil rolled his eyes.

He leaned closer to June, then jerked his head toward Grace. "Psstt," he said in a stage whisper, "Grace wants to know if you think I'm cute."

Grace buried her face in her hands. One corner of June's mouth quirked up, and the tightness in her face began to soften with the beginnings of a smile.

Phillip let himself start to smile back. He leaned back in his chair and crossed his arms over his chest. "Ah. Did the sun come out, or did you just smile at me?"

Still, she didn't speak. Almost as a mirror to his own position at the table, June crossed her arms and leaned back in her chair, watching him, smirking.

Phillip cleared his throat. "You know something? I lost my phone number. Can I have yours?"

Finally, she broke out into a genuine smile. Now that he saw it, she really did have a nice smile. With her smile, she finally spoke. "I don't know if there's any response to any of those bad pickup lines."

Phillip shrugged his shoulders. "There has to be, otherwise guys wouldn't use them."

On the other side of the table from Phillip, Neil groaned. "Forget the pickup lines. Did you see the last Blackhawks game? I wonder if they're going to make the play-offs this year."

Phillip continued to lean back in the chair with his arms crossed. He turned his head toward Neil. "I don't know if the ladies want to talk about the Blackhawks, Neil. Can't you forget about hockey for one day?"

Both of June's eyebrows rose. "It's okay, Phil. Next week they play the Kings on home ice. That should be an interesting game. What do you think, Neil?"

"I'm not much of a Kings fan myself. But those Canucks are looking really good this year, so far, anyway."

Phillip could have joined in, but he knew that Grace wasn't much into hockey. He didn't want to see her left out of the conversation.

Leaving Neil and June to discuss the possibilities of future play-off contenders, he turned to Grace. "Did Neil tell you that I've been learning to play guitar? That's one of the reasons I wanted to come tonight. One day I'd love to be good enough to play for our church's worship team. It's kind of a dream of mine. But for now, I just enjoy watching and listening to live musicians, especially Christian musicians. Who knows, maybe I can pick up some tips."

"Aren't you taking lessons?"

Phillip shook his head. "No. Do you know Tyler? He plays, but his schedule has been too erratic to plan regular lessons. So far he's been teaching me when we can get our schedules together. I've got this book, too, but it's not the same as sitting down with someone and actually being shown what I need to know. I'm not very good, but I'm making progress, so I guess that's what counts."

"I've played guitar for years. People have told me I'm pretty good. Maybe I can give you some pointers and a few lessons."

Phillip felt his heart stop beating for a split second. He'd been praying that he would find a way to spend more time with Grace without looking like he was tagging along with her and Neil like a lost puppy. Now God had provided a way to do that without stepping past the boundaries of her relationship with Neil, which Phillip found himself starting to struggle with.

He swallowed hard and hoped his voice came out normally. "That would be great. I didn't know you played guitar. I've been having trouble with the bar chord for—"

"Good evening, everyone!" a male voice boomed from the speakers overhead. "Praise the Lord for a full house tonight!"

A round of applause drowned out any opportunity he could have had to speak.

Everyone in attendance listened while a young man on stage gave the audience a summary of what led up to the opening of the coffeehouse. Next, he gave the audience a challenge, offering a prize for patrons to think up a name for the new venture by the end of the evening.

The lights dimmed, and another young man joined the first at the microphone. The first man gave the introductions about the musicians onstage, spoke about their upcoming CD, then expounded on how they would soon be branching out their ministry with their music.

The featured singer signaled the musicians, the emcee walked off the stage, and then the music began.

Rather than being rude and trying to speak over the music, Phillip settled into his chair to enjoy the show and study the guitarists, which was the primary reason he had wanted to come in the first place.

However, suddenly his secondary reason for being there had become more important than the first.

Grace.

While he watched the singer, he thought of the previous Sunday, when he'd sat beside Grace in church. She sang every bit as good as the man on stage, with the obvious gender difference. If she played guitar as well as she sang, he could only imagine the combination and anticipated the day he could hear her for himself. Naturally he would ask her to sing while she played something for him during a guitar lesson. But, to take that one step further, her ability to play guitar and sing well presented countless ministry opportunities.

He knew she would never stand at the front of the church to sing and play guitar, but there were many other ways to use her talent for the Lord's work. Youth-group functions. Ladies' ministry functions. He wondered why she wasn't in the church choir, as her absence was a definite loss to the congregation.

During a quiet moment in one of the songs, something brushed him. He turned his head to see Grace's small hand resting on his forearm.

Instead of staring at her hand, he raised his head to look at her face, which was a mistake.

Her adorable smile and warm, brown eyes did funny things to his stomach.

Very gently, she gave his arm a gentle squeeze. The warmth of her hand nearly burned him, even through the fabric of his shirt. His pulse started beating erratically.

"They're really good, and I'm having a wonderful time. This was a great idea. Thanks."

Despite the warmth of the large room, Phil broke out in a cold sweat. A couple of days ago, something strange had come over him, and he'd wanted to kiss Grace. He'd shaken it off as a bout of temporary insanity. Except, the insanity had returned. He wanted to kiss her again.

If they hadn't been in a public place...

And if she wasn't dating his best friend...

The sweet latte in his stomach suddenly turned sour and went to war with the pretzels he'd been nibbling.

Phillip shook his head, then nodded. "You're welcome," he said, his voice coming out like someone was squeezing his throat. But it wasn't his throat being squeezed. It was his heart.

He was falling for his best friend's girlfriend.

The realization of what was happening hit him like a ton of bricks.

"Phil? Are you okay? You look funny all of a sudden."

His throat constricted, but he forced himself to speak past it. "Yeah, I'm fine. Maybe this coffee is too hot or something."

Her brows knotted like she obviously didn't believe him. "If you need to go home, that's okay. I don't mind, and I'm sure Neil and June won't mind either."

"I'm okay. Really."

The song ended, and the audience gave the band a rousing round of applause, sparing him from having to respond.

Phillip clapped along numbly.

Grace's concern for his health drove another nail into his heart. Throughout his life, through his own experience and the experiences of his friends, Phillip had thought there was nothing more pathetic than falling for someone who didn't feel the same way. Now, he knew different. Not only was Grace obviously not interested in him the same way as he was, she was in love with someone else. And it couldn't have been just anyone. She was in love with his best friend.

What made the whole thing more disturbing was that he'd walked into the situation with his eyes wide open. He'd been perfectly aware of the relationship between Neil and Grace from the first time he'd started spending so much time with Grace.

Whether Neil realized it or not, Phillip now understood why Neil never brought Grace over to their place when he was home or why Neil didn't encourage Phillip to socialize with them. The potential for disaster had been there all along.

Likewise, Grace had been right to invite her friend along. Unfortunately, meeting June when he had was apparently too little, too late. Not that he didn't like June; she just wasn't Grace.

The lead singer didn't give the audience time to wind down their applause. Instead, he encouraged everyone present to stand and join in with the band on a contemporary chorus and an old hymn done in a way Phillip had never heard before.

As the song ended, the music quieted, and the leader encouraged anyone present who wanted to receive Christ into their hearts to come forward. Phillip had experienced invitations for new believers to come forward at his church often, but he had never seen them being made at what was mostly a social gathering. Therefore he didn't know what to expect.

The whole place was charged with emotion when a number of people stepped forward. A surge of joy tightened his chest, even though he didn't know a single one of God's newest children. He wanted to say something to Neil, but he found he couldn't speak.

Beside him came the sound of a sniffle.

He turned his head to see Grace, tears streaming down her face. "This is so beautiful," she choked out. "Isn't it wonderful?"

Her tears of joy drove another nail into his heart. He wanted to take her and wrap his arms around her and hold her while she cried, as a way to share the heady moment with her.

But he couldn't. She belonged to someone else. To his best friend.

"Here." Neil reached to the center of the table, pulled a napkin out of the holder, and handed it to Grace. "I think you'd better blow your nose." As she leaned forward to blow, Neil put one arm around her shoulder. "Feel better?"

Grace nodded, still holding the napkin in front of her nose. "Yes. Thanks, Neil."

It suddenly occurred to Phillip that perhaps he should have been checking on June, who was officially his date. When he turned to June, her eyes were glassy, but she wasn't crying.

She sniffled delicately, then rubbed her eyes with her fingers. "That was really neat. I guess we'd better go. We all have to be up early for church in the morning."

Phillip nodded but said nothing. Going to church with Neil and Grace was going to be difficult enough, but sometime after church, he and Grace had plans to once more fix Dale.

This time, Phillip told himself that, no matter what, he would have Neil present. And, after Dale was fixed for the last time, he wouldn't allow himself to see Grace again until he had his errant brain cells under control.

Chapter 9

"Grace? Neil wasn't expecting you. He's not home."

Grace smiled. "That's okay, Phil. I'm not here to see Neil. I'm here to see you."

His face paled, which strengthened her concern that something was wrong.

Yesterday after church, all three of them had gone to her apartment to restarch Phil's Christmas angel. Nothing specific had been said, and it was nothing she could put her finger on, but all day she'd had the feeling something was wrong. Neil had been the same as he always was, but Phil had been different—uncharacteristically quiet and unusually serious. The same as the evening before at the coffeehouse, she'd asked him if he was feeling sick, but he claimed he was fine. She didn't think he was, but she couldn't call him a liar.

To make matters worse, when she'd offered to make coffee after they'd finished their project, not only had he turned her down, he'd also been in a rush to leave.

She had to know why. If it was something she'd said or done to upset him, she'd never forgive herself.

"Sorry to drop by unexpectedly. I tried to call, but I forgot to charge the battery on my cell phone. I decided to take a chance that you were home, and here you are."

She stood in the doorway, waiting.

Phil also stood in the doorway. He wouldn't look at her. Instead, he peeked over her shoulder at her car parked on the street, then up into the night sky, to the bag in her hand, then down to her guitar, which rested at her feet on the porch.

She held out the bag. "I brought Dale. I put her over the heat vent last night, and she was dry when I got home from work today."

"That's great. Thanks." He reached out and accepted the bag. "I'm being so rude. Please come in."

She bent down to grasp the handle of her guitar case and followed him in, shutting the door behind herself.

"You brought your guitar."

Grace grinned. "Brilliant observation, Sherlock."

"Why?"

"Saturday you said you were learning to play. I was at my friend's house for supper, and I had my guitar with me, so I thought I'd make a pit stop on my way home and give you an impromptu lesson. I also wanted to give Dale back as soon as possible."

"That's really nice of you, but after I said that, I started thinking that maybe taking lessons from you might not be such a great idea."

Her hands faltered on the latch of the guitar case, but she recovered and continued to remove the guitar from the case. "Why not? I think it's a great idea. It's not like I'm going to charge you money or anything. I've been thinking recently that maybe I could teach lessons to make a little extra pocket money. This is a good way to see if I'm cut out to be a teacher. You don't mind me using you as a guinea pig, do you?"

"Uh, well, I guess not. I suppose I should go put Dale down and get my guitar."

He set Dale carefully in the center of the coffee table, paused, then smiled for a brief second as he gently ran his fingers over Dale's delicate blond hair.

"I'll be right back," he said and walked down the hallway toward his bedroom.

While Phil was gone, Grace made herself comfortable on the new couch. She'd heard about the addition of furniture to their living room, first from Phil, then from Neil. Phil had been correct. The room was just on the verge of feeling overcrowded, but the two men had done an admirable job of arranging everything to make it fit. She could well imagine both of them in the room, each one stretched out on a couch, watching television together.

Phil returned with a polished black guitar and a small Fender amp.

"I should have known you'd have an electric guitar. Mine's an acoustic. I don't require electricity to play."

"I guess it's a guy thing." For a split second, Phil smiled. It was good to see the old Phil back, even if it was only for a moment. He positioned the amp on the other side of the coffee table, then sat beside her and picked up his guitar. "There's not much room in here. Good thing my amp is small and I've got a long patch cord."

"Can I see the book you're using? That would give me a good idea of where you are in the learning curve."

"Oh. Good idea." Phil stood, leaned the guitar against the couch, and once more disappeared into his bedroom.

As she waited, Grace thought about the last time she'd been in the same room and the differences beyond the obvious extra furniture.

Almost every other time she'd been at Neil and Phil's

house, it had been when Phil wasn't home. Today, instead of the television blaring, soft music played in the background. A book lay open and pressed down, displaying the title of a current mystery by a popular Christian author.

Before she could read the back cover completely, Phil returned, a book and a stack of paper in his hand. "Here it is. I also printed a bunch of stuff off the Internet. Some of these are songs we do in church on Sunday morning. But like I said before, I'm not very good yet."

"We all have to start somewhere," Grace mumbled as she paged through his book. "The first thing we should do is tune up together. I'm not going to make you get up again. I brought my own tuning meter."

As it turned out, Phil did have to get up again, but this time only to unplug his patch cord from the amp into the meter while he tuned his guitar. They both laughed when he got up to plug the guitar into the amp again, then one more time to turn off his CD player so they could begin for real.

Grace moved Dale aside on the coffee table to make room for the book and all the music, then pushed the book toward Phil. "Let's start by playing this one. Are there any chords here you don't know?"

"No, I'm fine with that one."

His playing was a little choppy, but nothing a little practice and confidence wouldn't fix. They worked through a couple of lessons, and even in the short time they were together, Grace could already see an improvement.

When they were done, Grace couldn't help but smile when Phil shook his left hand in the air.

"Ouch. I can both see and feel the lines the strings have dug into my fingers. I think I need to work on my calluses a little more."

"Regular practice will cure that. And regular lessons.

What do you say we set aside every Monday evening? It seems to be a time when neither of us makes other plans."

"I don't know if that's such a good idea, Grace."

His words sent a chill into her heart. All day long she'd wondered what she'd said or done to hurt him. Trying to imagine all was fine and bringing over her guitar may have broken the ice for a couple of hours, but it had not gotten rid of the problem like she had hoped, obviously unrealistically.

She'd thought and thought about it all day and couldn't come up with any good reason why he'd been acting so strangely. Usually confrontations terrified her, but she couldn't figure this one out for herself, no matter how hard she tried. This time, she had no alternative but to ask him what was wrong. Otherwise, she risked letting the problem fester until it was past the point of healing. She couldn't let that happen with Phil.

The risk involved completely outweighed her fear of facing him, even if the answer hurt. Earlier, he'd expressed the view that he didn't want to take guitar lessons from her. She hadn't given him a chance to respond; she'd barged in and given him the lesson whether he'd wanted it or not. She couldn't believe she possessed such courage or such gall, except that she'd actually done it.

But now, the moment of truth had come.

Grace swallowed hard, then forced herself to smile. All she could say was, "Why not?"

"You know. Because of Neil. And stuff."

A wave of relief surged through her. Whatever was bothering him wasn't her, even though she didn't quite know what it really was.

She summoned what little was left of her courage and looked him straight in the eye, even though the effort almost hurt. "Can you define 'stuff'?"

He swiped one hand through his hair, then folded his

hands tightly in his lap. "Lately you've been seeing more of me than you have been of Neil."

"Is that all? Don't worry about Neil. He doesn't mind. We've had extenuating circumstances with Dale getting damaged, so that was just temporary. Besides, I don't have to account to him for every minute of my time. It's not like we're married or anything. And even if we were, he wouldn't be my lord and keeper. This is the twenty-first century, after all."

Phil's eyes widened. "Do you think you might get married someday?"

"I…" Grace let her voice trail off. She didn't know how he knew, but she had been thinking of marriage recently. In the back of her mind, she wondered if it all started the day they named Dale. On that day, Phil had mentioned that he was thinking about settling down, and she had started to think of the possibilities of one day getting married herself. Because of that, since their outing Saturday night, when she hadn't been thinking about what she could have done to hurt Phil's feelings, she'd been thinking of the possibilities for Phil and June. She hadn't yet talked to June, but she couldn't see June not liking Phil, considering how much she liked him.

"I think most single people my age think about marriage, women probably more than men."

Suddenly, Phil stood. "Neil should be back soon. Would you like it if I made a pot of coffee?"

Grace stood as well. "I'll help."

Phil's weak smile sent shivers to her heart. "I don't think it's a lot of work to put on a pot of coffee, but if you want to risk seeing my messy kitchen, that's fine with me."

The kitchen wasn't as bad as she imagined it could be for two single men living together, especially having dropped in unannounced, although it wasn't tidy by any stretch of the imagination.

Not a word was said as Phil dumped out the old grounds, inserted a new filter, and began to measure the new coffee.

Grace leaned against the wall and crossed her arms, hoping to look relaxed when she was feeling anything but. For a few seconds she held her breath while she summoned her courage to ask the next question. "I have to ask you something. What did you think of June?"

"She seemed nice, I guess."

Grace waited for him to say more, but he didn't. He simply flicked the switch on the coffeemaker and turned around. "Done. Want to go back to the living room?"

"Sure."

Grace parked herself on the new couch while Phil selected a different CD and dropped it into the tray. "I just got this new praise CD last week. I think you'll like it. It's really good."

When the music began to play, Phil adjusted the volume until it was at a comfortable level. He then sat at the opposite end of the other couch, leaving what Grace thought was a vast chasm for such a small room.

He hadn't been down for more than three seconds before he stood again. "I just thought of something. It's good to have Dale home again, but even during something so simple, Dale really was in the way. I'm going to move him, and what better place than on top of the television? It's out of the way, it's safer than on top of the coffee table, and it's also a good spot to display him as a central point of reference in the room."

Grace watched Phil's every move as he picked Dale up, walked across the room, then carefully positioned Dale just right, perfectly centered, on top of the television.

He stood back and crossed his arms. "There. What do you think?"

Abruptly, Grace sat upright. "That's what the difference is in here! The television!"

Phil blinked and knotted his brows, but otherwise didn't move. "We moved the television, yes, but we moved around pretty much everything in the whole room since you've last been here. Maybe it just feels different with Dale on top. He does kind of cheer things up in here. Kind of like an angelic aura or something."

Grace shook her head and waved one hand in the air in the direction of the television. "No, you don't understand. It's not Dale; it's the television itself. It's not on. That's why the room feels so different. Even though it's all been rearranged, it's the same furniture with the exception of the new couch, which I've heard about many times. The difference is the noise level. Neil always has the television on, even when we're really not watching it."

Phil nodded. "Yeah. I know. I've taught myself to ignore it when Neil does that, at least most of the time. When I'm alone and there's nothing on that I'm specifically watching, I turn off the television and put on some music. I can't say it's less noisy, though. Sometimes I crank the volume pretty high."

"Maybe, but steady music is different than the blare of voices and the blasting of special effects with loud bursts of short bits of instrumentals for emphasis on the action at the time. No matter how good the show might be, if you're not watching it, it's just noise. Sometimes I wish I could turn up the volume on my CD player, too, but living in an apartment block, I don't have that option without bothering my neighbors."

"One day you'll have a house, and you can put it up as loud as you want. If you want, I can turn it up real loud for you right now."

He moved as if he were going to stand and actually do it. Grace suspected he was only kidding, but she raised her palms to stop him anyway, just in case. "That's okay! I didn't mean now."

Phil grinned. "Relax. I was just getting up to go pour the coffee." He gave her an exaggerated wink over his shoulder as he left the room. "Gotcha."

Grace smiled. The old Phil was back, and she liked it that way.

"Maybe I'll just stay here and let you serve me," she called out. "You know how I like my coffee by now."

In three minutes flat, he was back with a mug of coffee, just the way she liked it.

She told herself that if Neil hadn't arrived by nine-thirty, she would leave. To her surprise, at ten o'clock, there was no sign of Neil, and she was still there, still talking to Phil.

Since she had to get up at 7:10 to be on time for work, Grace excused herself. Phil saw her to the door and waited while she pulled on her boots and slipped into her coat.

"It's going to be a strange week with Thanksgiving on Thursday, then going back to work on Friday. I'm going to my parents' home, and it's a long drive back for me after a big supper, and always a late night. I'm always wiped out on Friday, which tends to be busy, as so many people have the day off. I wish I had more seniority at the bank and could book the day off."

"I know what you mean. I can never get the Friday off either. I always go to Granny's place for Thanksgiving. This Thanksgiving is going to be really different because she's moved into her apartment, but she wants to still have everyone over just like every other year. It's always been important to her to have all the big holiday family dinners at her house, and it's really upset her that she can't anymore due to lack of space. We're all going to try to fit into her small apartment for one last Thanksgiving, but starting this Christmas, my parents are going to host all the family dinner occasions. It feels really strange, but I guess all families go through this when a tradition passes on to the next generation."

"Yes, I think you're right." Grace hiked her purse over her shoulder and reached down to pick up her guitar. "I was a child when my grandparents died, but it still felt very different the first time my parents hosted a family dinner. Suddenly things changed from the whole extended family to it just being our own family. Of course, now that my sister is married and has kids, the family is getting larger again, just one generation down."

"Oops, wait for a sec. I forgot something."

She lowered the guitar to the floor while Phil disappeared into the kitchen for a few seconds.

"I forgot to give you this yesterday." He held out her travel coffee mug that she'd loaned him the night Ralphie attacked poor Dale. "I would have filled it up, but having more coffee so close to bedtime probably isn't a good idea."

"Probably not," she said as she reached out to take it from him. As she wrapped her fingers around it, he didn't release it. Instead, his left hand covered her right, sandwiching her hand between his and the plastic mug.

"Drive safely; it's slippery in places," he murmured. "Thanks for coming. I really enjoyed this evening."

Mesmerized by his eyes, Grace stood frozen, completely unable to move. "Y-yes," she stammered. "Me, too."

"Good night, Grace."

All she had to do was move and he would have released her hand. She couldn't. The heat of his hand seeped into hers as she stared up into his limpid gray-green eyes. Eyes that said so much. Eyes that said he might kiss her goodbye.

Grace yanked the mug out of his grasp, backed up, and picked up her guitar case in one brusque motion. "Yes. Good night, Phil." She turned around so fast, the neck of the guitar case bumped the door frame on her way out.

She was halfway to her car when Neil's pickup pulled into the driveway.

The driver's door opened, and Neil slid out just as Grace opened her own driver's door.

"Grace? Is that you?"

"Hi, Neil," she mumbled over top of her car. "Sorry I missed you. It's really late-I-have-to-go-bye."

She nearly threw her guitar and purse across the driver's seat and into the passenger seat, slid in, and turned the key, all before Neil arrived beside her door. He tapped on the window with his gloved fingertips, so she had no alternative but to roll the window down while her car warmed up.

"What are you doing here?"

"Nothing, really. Wouldn't you know it, you'd come when I finally gave up."

Neil straightened, pushed the cuff of his glove away from his wrist, then he tilted his wrist to catch the light from the streetlight. "Oh. I didn't know it was so late. Sorry I missed you. I guess I'll see you Wednesday."

"Probably. Good night, Neil."

"Good night, Grace."

Without first leaning in through her open car window to give her a good night kiss or even a token peck on the cheek, Neil backed up, turned, and walked into the house, leaving her alone in the driveway.

Grace stared at the closed door while she waited for her engine to warm up sufficiently.

Neil didn't try to kiss her good night. It didn't look like he even wanted to. In fact, she could count on one hand the number of times he'd kissed her good night in the past month.

On the other hand, Phil had looked like he had wanted to kiss her good night. His gorgeous eyes had almost looked like he was in pain because he didn't, except Grace knew that couldn't have been the case—she knew she'd completely misread him.

But if that was what he was thinking, and he had tried to kiss her, Grace wasn't sure she would have pushed him away.

Grace blinked hard, tore her gaze from Neil and Phil's house, and turned her concentration to where it should have been, which was driving home.

Safely. Just as Phil had said.

Chapter 10

The door creaked open and banged shut. Two thuds echoed down the hall as Neil's boots bumped the wall when he kicked them off. At the same time, Neil's voice drifted through the house. "What was Grace doing here?"

Phillip sucked in a deep breath as he tucked his guitar back into the case. Very slowly, he pushed his amp into the corner of his bedroom. He wasn't ready to talk about Grace, especially to Neil.

He'd acted like a moron. When he opened the door and saw Grace on the porch, waiting to be invited in, all he could do was stand there with his mouth hanging open. Without Neil being there, part of him wanted to see her, and part of him didn't. Since he had to make a decision, he let her in, first because she'd done him a favor by bringing Dale, and second, because she'd also come to do him another favor with the guitar lesson.

Once they settled in together and actually started the guitar lesson, all, not part of him, didn't want Neil to come home.

At first he was so tense he couldn't think straight, but Grace was so gentle and patient with her instructions that he soon forgot himself and his nervousness. By the time the lesson ended and they sat back to talk, he'd relaxed so much that the evening disappeared as if it had only been minutes, when in fact she'd been there nearly three hours.

He didn't know what was happening, and he didn't know if he liked it. When they weren't together, he seemed to spend most of his time, including free moments at work, thinking of her. When they were together, he was torn between wanting to hold her tight and kiss her and wanting to run for the hills.

He'd never been so confused in his life.

"There you are. I said, what was Grace doing here?"

Phillip spun around on his toes. Neil stood in the doorway with his arms crossed over his chest, waiting for a response.

Phillip struggled to think of something to say. He didn't know when it happened, but he'd crossed some kind of line, even though he couldn't determine where the boundaries lay.

All he knew was that he was in way over his head. Common sense told him he needed some distance from Grace, but his heart told him not to let her go; he simply liked her too much.

Nothing they did was hurting anyone. Grace's relationship with Neil hadn't changed, nor had Phillip's friendship with Neil. As Grace proclaimed, Neil didn't seem to mind him spending so much time with Grace. In fact, many times Phillip had not only encouraged Neil to come with him to Grace's apartment, Phillip had insisted Neil come when Neil really hadn't wanted to go. It almost seemed that Phillip valued the relationship between Neil and Grace more than Neil did.

Phillip cleared his throat and stared pointedly into Neil's

eyes. "She brought Granny's angel back, plus she gave me a guitar lesson. We waited for you for a long time. When you didn't show, she gave up and left. It was past her bedtime, anyway. Where were you?"

"I was at Tyler's. We got carried away, I guess, and lost track of the time. So how are you coming with that guitar? Can you make music yet?"

Neil turned and walked into the living room, so Phillip followed him.

"I'm working on it. I'd really like to get the chord chart for that new song we did last Sunday and try to figure it out. Do you remember the name?"

Once in the living room, Neil picked up the remote from the coffee table and aimed it at the television, then lowered it again before he hit the power button. "Very funny, putting your angel on top of the television."

"I figured that's where it's the safest."

Neil again aimed the remote at the television, but Phillip spoke out, once again stopping him from pushing the button.

"Why do you need to turn the television on now? Look at the time. Nothing's on; it's almost bedtime."

"I want to watch the news."

"You never watch the news. You turn it on, then go into the kitchen and make yourself something to eat. By the time you come out, the news is over and twenty-year-old reruns are on."

Finally Neil pushed the button, but the television remained off. "Hmm…" he mumbled, then pushed the button again, but with the same result. "What's going on?"

Phillip felt a smile tugging at the corners of his mouth, and he couldn't stop it. While Neil stood, stone-faced, turning the remote over in his hand, Phillip couldn't stop his grin from turning into a smile, then to a muffled chuckle, until he broke out into a full laugh. "Grace took the batteries out!" he choked out between gasps. Picturing Grace giggling as she removed the batteries and hid them under the couch cushion, Phillip laughed so hard he had to press one hand into his ribs.

Neil didn't laugh. He didn't even crack a smile. The battery-less remote control still in his hand, his arm fell to his side. "She did what?"

Phillip wiped his eyes as his laughter wound down. "I said she took the batteries out. We both thought you watch too much television, so she decided to do something about it."

"Grace would never do something like that. You set her up."

Phillip couldn't hold back his grin. "I didn't. In fact, it was her idea."

"That's not possible."

"I don't know why you think she's so shy, Neil. She may take awhile to really make up her mind on something, but once she does, she can really be a force to be reckoned with."

"I think you're a bad influence on her."

Phillip shook his head. "Not true. She also said that instead of sitting on the couch watching all that hockey, you should be outside, playing hockey."

Neil blinked and stared blankly.

"That's right. She even suggested that this weekend the three of us should go skating."

"I haven't been on skates in years. Neither have you."

"Neither has she, but that isn't going to stop her. She said she's going to borrow skates from a friend, wear double socks, and we're all going skating on Saturday afternoon."

"I don't believe this."

"Believe it."

Neil waved the remote back and forth in front of himself, then ended up pointing it at Phillip. "Didn't you have anything to say while she was making all these plans?"

Phillip shrugged his shoulders. "What could I say? I agreed with her. We all need more exercise, and you watch too much television. Loosen up. You might have some fun."

"But…" Neil's voice trailed off.

Before Neil could recover, Phillip turned around, speaking over his shoulder as he walked away. "See you sometime tomorrow. It's late and I'm going to bed. Night."

Phillip pushed the buzzer for Grace's apartment and waited, hoping he'd arrived early enough before she had to leave for her weekly Bible study meeting.

Grace's distorted voice blaring through the cheap speaker did funny things to his stomach, but he told himself that it was only because he was too hungry, since he'd come straight from work and hadn't stopped for supper.

He leaned closer, although he knew he didn't have to. "Grace, it's me. Phil. I'm really sorry, but I need your help…."

Even through the static, he could feel the silence hang before she finally told him to come up and pushed the button for the buzzer.

Just like every other time he visited, when he stepped out of the elevator, Grace awaited him in the hall in front of her apartment door. Immediately on seeing him, her eyebrows knotted and her gaze dropped to his hands, which were empty. As he walked closer, her eyebrows quirked up, and she met his eyes.

Not wanting to keep her in suspense, he spoke as soon as he was close enough to speak without raising his voice. "It's Dale," he said as he reached into his coat pocket. "I'm afraid I had a little accident."

Her mouth dropped open. "Dale is in your pocket? It's

that bad?" She pressed both palms to her cheeks. "What happened?"

He gave her a one-sided smile. "Don't worry, it's not that terminal that he's all squished up and rammed into my pocket. It's just the halo."

Once inside her apartment, he pulled the small plastic bag out of his pocket while Grace closed the door behind them.

"I've got to give you my excuse first because I'm trying to make myself feel not so stupid. I thought the halo looked a little lopsided. You know, we've taken it off a couple of times, and he's been moved around a lot lately. So I thought, it's a piece of wire the beads are strung on, right? I should be able to bend it back into shape easily, right? I tried to bend it with my fingers, but I couldn't get the kink out, so I took my needle-nosed pliers and tried to get between a couple of the beads to press the wire flat. I must have pressed too hard, or the width of the pliers put too much pressure on where it's twisted together or something, because the thing snapped. I knew the beads were small, but I really didn't know how small until I had to look for them. I think some rolled down the heat vent, and I think some slipped in that little space where the carpet ends when it hits the wall. I'm sure there are some that I couldn't find when I tried to pick them out of the carpet. I'll probably hear them getting sucked up when I vacuum."

Grace squeezed her eyes shut, lowered her head, and pressed into her brow with her index finger and thumb. Phillip didn't think it was a good sign.

He held up the plastic bag containing the broken wire and remains of the beads he could find and cleared his throat to continue. "I did manage to recover this many, but it's not enough to make a whole halo again. I need you to go shopping with me. I have no idea where to find this stuff."

"Those are Indian beads, and they're only available in select craft shops and specialty bead stores. But even of the few stores in town that actually carry a good selection of Indian beads, there is no way in the world you're ever going to match up fifty-year-old beads. There's dye lots to consider, and I know they're glass, but they might have faded with age, too."

"I thought of that. But certainly we can buy beads that are colored so they *look* fifty years old. All we have to do is match the color, and no one will know the difference, right? I already looked online, but I can't get an accurate match because every monitor has a default color setting of its own from the manufacturer, and every brand is different. Besides, I don't have the time to wait for shipping and then risk the chance it doesn't match and having to go through it all again. Thanksgiving is tomorrow, and the Christmas shopping rush has already begun. I have to do this in person."

"This is Wednesday. Nothing is open tonight. Tomorrow is Thanksgiving, and Friday not every place will be open. The major stores will soon be staying open late every night until Christmas, but I'm not sure about specialty shops like that, because they're not holiday driven. I think the only thing we can do is go shopping Saturday. That means we'll have to postpone our skating day for another weekend. By the way, what did Neil say?"

Phillip broke out into a wide grin. "He was really surprised that you suggested skating. But I think he was even more surprised about the batteries."

Grace also broke out into a grin. "I wish I could have seen his face."

A small chuckle escaped him. "I can't remember the last time I laughed so hard. It was like he went into shock."

"But do you think he took the hint? We weren't exactly subtle."

"Don't give me this 'we' stuff, Grace. It was your idea, not mine. All I did was show you how to open it. You're the one who hid the batteries."

"You know what I meant. Will it make a difference?"

Phillip opened his mouth, but instead of his voice, the only sound in the room was his grumbling stomach.

The heat of his blush spread from his neck to his forehead. He pressed both hands into his stomach. "Oops. Excuse me."

"I guess I don't have to ask if you've had supper. I don't mind making you a sandwich. I made a roast beef for supper, and there's always more than I can eat by myself. It's a pleasure not to waste it."

Before he could pretend to protest, Grace turned and walked into the kitchen, so he followed.

Rather than sit down at the table and wait for her to serve him, Phillip stood beside Grace as she opened the freezer to bring out a bag of buns. "I feel strange not doing anything. I didn't come here so you could feed me, although I won't complain. Your cooking is bound to be better than mine. I know it's got to be better than Neil's. You wouldn't believe some of the things he tries to pass off as edible."

He paused, expecting and even anticipating Grace to make a sarcastic remark about the two of them trying to put together a decent meal, especially since she had to know the disaster Neil could be in the kitchen. Instead, she stopped slicing the meat and lowered her head.

Her voice came out so quiet he could barely hear her, even though they were side by side. "I wouldn't care if the meals were less than perfect. It's better than eating alone every day."

Despite the fragrance of the bun just out of the microwave and the mouthwatering aroma of the warm, freshly sliced roast beef in front of him, Phillip's appetite disappeared. While Neil wasn't family, and living with Neil was far from living with the perfect wife, Phillip was never truly alone. He'd never really been alone.

After he graduated from high school, he and Neil decided to live on campus while attending college and, as best friends, they had roomed together. When they graduated from college, it had only been natural that they continue their living arrangements. Both of them had found jobs immediately, so they rented a house together and had been sharing the same house ever since.

Over the years they had settled into a comfortable routine. Some days they barely saw each other except for the morning rush over the coffeepot and getting out the door on time for work. Other days they spent the evening together in the living room. Most days, though, despite plans and activities, they at least ate supper together.

The bottom line was that no matter what their schedules were like and whether they did anything together over the course of a day or not, they were always there for each other, even if, at times, it only meant sleeping under the same roof. He always had someone to turn to when he needed a friend, and likewise, so did Neil.

He didn't know much about Grace's background, only that her parents lived in a small town not too far away. Still, it wasn't close enough that Grace saw them very often. In order to find a job, Grace had moved out of her parents' home and away from all her childhood friends to live in the city with her sister about five years ago. That had lasted about a year, until her sister announced her pending engagement. Grace moved out on her own and had been living alone ever since.

Even though Neil sometimes drove him nuts, he could well imagine how lonely it could be to live alone. Thinking of Grace being lonely drove a knife through his heart. He didn't want her to be lonely or sad. The sadness in Grace's voice made him want to reach out and touch her, to wind his fingers in her soft, flowing hair, to hold her in his arms and rest her head against his heart and take the pain out of her big, brown eyes.

But he didn't have that right. Whatever rights he could claim were those of a friend—and a friend only. The way he wanted to hold her was more than simple friendship. Much more.

Phillip rammed his hands in his pockets. "Neil may be a rotten cook, and I'm not much better, but if you're willing to take the chance, you're more than welcome to join us every once in awhile. In fact, I'd welcome the chance to eat a decent meal now and then. Just be warned. We'd expect you to take your turn at doing dishes."

Her weak smile drove the knife in a little deeper.

"Thank you. I didn't mean to sound like such a sad sack, but I might just take you up on that, although you may not want me. I'm not a very good cook either."

He tried to smile, but he knew he looked as lame as he felt. "Then the three of us would be in good company together."

"Here's your sandwich."

"Thanks."

Because Grace wasn't eating, Phillip closed his eyes for a couple of seconds of silent prayer, then took a big, big bite. He paused mid-chew to savor the flavor. Instead of using a processed cheese slice, Grace had tucked some fresh cheese inside, which between the heated bun and the warm meat had become delightfully soft but not melted. It would have been polite to make small talk while he ate, but the best he could do was to grunt his responses between bites.

Adding fresh cheese was nothing he hadn't done before, but this was the best sandwich he'd tasted in his life. The reason was because Grace had made it, and she'd made it just for him.

And with that thought, Phillip knew he was in big trouble.

He couldn't help it. When he was done the last bite, he let out a rather contented sigh. "That was great. Thank you, Grace."

She smiled so sweetly, he felt as soft and mushy as the cheese he'd just eaten.

She looked down for a second to check her watch. "I don't mean to be rude, but it's time to leave for my Bible study meeting. I guess you know that Neil had to work late tonight, so he can't come. I don't know which group you usually go to, but if you want, you're welcome to come with me. Just pretend you're Neil."

At the word "pretend," Phillip's world shifted.

For the past week, maybe more, that was exactly what he had been doing.

Pretending.

He'd been pretending that he could be friends with Grace, and he wasn't good at pretending. He wanted more than mere friendship. Much more. But he couldn't do more, because that was up to Neil.

If he was going to pretend to be Neil, then he would do what he suspected Neil wasn't doing, and that would be to put all else aside and spend more time with Grace. Already, her hurts were becoming his hurts, and he was starting to go to ridiculous lengths to make her smile when he thought she needed it.

There had been a few serious girlfriends in Phillip's life, but lately he'd been experiencing something that had never happened before. When he wasn't with Grace, he missed her. He was no longer content to simply wait until the weekend when he would see her in church, at a distance. He wanted to be with her, and not only to spend time in the same room with her—he wanted to touch her and cherish her and make her happy to be with him, too.

That would be the way it was if he were Neil, but he wasn't Neil, nor could he pretend to be. Of course he knew Grace had only been joking, but Grace's significance in his life was no longer a joking matter.

To pretend to be Neil would be wrong. He needed to do the opposite—to spend less time with Grace. He had to step back to let Neil spend more time with her. Once already he had decided not to spend so much time with her, but all it took was for her to show up on his doorstep, and all his good intentions flew out the window.

As time went on, the more he saw Neil and Grace together, the less he could figure out their relationship or their level of commitment to each other. However, if they were happy together, it was not his place to judge.

The only solution could be that, after tonight, he wouldn't see Grace anymore. Otherwise, he was only setting himself up for future heartbreak.

"Come on, Phil. We should go now."

He opened his mouth to tell her he'd changed his mind, but the warmth in her big, brown eyes stopped him. He couldn't risk that he'd hurt her feelings when he was unable to explain his reasons for not going when he'd already said he would.

Therefore, after tonight, he wouldn't see her again.

Rather than reply, he followed her to the door, where they put their coats and boots on.

Grace carefully locked the door, and they made their way down the hall toward the elevator. "Oh, about Saturday. I think Neil wants to go back to that coffeehouse. We both had a really nice time. Why don't you pick me up after lunch? We'll go to a few places to find the right beads, and then all three of us can do something for supper together. Then Neil won't have to pick me up. I'll already be at your house when it's time to go to the coffeehouse. If you want to come, I'm sure Neil would like that. I can even ask June if she wants to come again. I know she had a good time."

For some reason, the movement of the elevator set off the delicious sandwich he'd just eaten, something that had never happened to him before. At the same time, he'd also suffered significant memory loss. The reason he'd come to see Grace today was to do something about the missing beads. Already, he'd forgotten that they had made plans to go shopping together.

He couldn't avoid doing the shopping, but he didn't have to sit at the same table with Neil and Grace on Saturday night and watch them hold hands and stare into each other's eyes. Even though he hadn't witnessed such behavior yet, there was nothing to say that it wouldn't start on Saturday night. If it did, he couldn't take it. "Sorry, Grace. I think I'm going to pass this time. I have something else I'm going to be doing Saturday night."

"Oh. Okay."

Phillip gritted his teeth as he held the elevator door open for Grace to exit ahead of him.

The only thing he knew he would be doing on Saturday night was sitting home alone, stewing, because she was going to be out with Neil.

He was no longer sure he liked the idea.

Phillip shook his head.

For now, they were going to the Bible study. For the rest of the night, he was going to put thoughts of Grace and Neil out of his head.

Maybe.

Chapter 11

Grace placed the two beads on the counter side by side. This was the third craft store they'd tried, and the last on her list, but this time, it appeared they were successful. "I think this is the best match we're going to get, Phil. It's not exact, but the variance is so slight that I don't think anyone would notice."

Phil's expression was almost comical as he studied the two beads. "I can see the difference. The new ones are a bit lighter, but I think you're right. If they're not side by side, no one would be able to see they're not the same. Besides, Dale is going to be on top of the tree. No one is going to be studying the color variations of the halo, not even Granny."

Grace stepped back and Phil raised his head toward the clerk. "We'll take them," he said. "And a spool of that wire."

He reached into his pocket for his wallet and opened it while the clerk scooped the beads back into the plastic tube and rang up the sale. When the clerk told him the total price, his eyebrows went up, he tucked his credit card back into his wallet, and paid with cash.

When the door closed behind them and they were out of the store, he turned to her. "I can't believe that's all they cost. I was expecting to pay much more."

Grace shrugged her shoulders. "It's only a tube of beads. They're not expensive, really. They're just hard to find unless you know where to look."

"Which, of course, you did. Thanks, Grace. I don't know what I would have done without you this time and every other time something happened to poor Dale. You've been my knight in shining armor through this whole fiasco."

"I don't think there is such a thing as a female knight. Female angels, yes, but not knights."

His little lopsided grin did strange things to her stomach. "I don't think I want to go there."

She couldn't help but grin back, not because Phil's grin was doing funny things to her insides, but because his grin only added to the charm of the rest of the day. She didn't particularly like shopping, but shopping with Phil had become an experience like no other.

Not many men hung out at the local craft shops. The few she'd seen today were very obviously with their wives, either there to watch children while their wives selected the items needed, or they had been reluctantly dragged inside rather than waiting outside on a cold winter day. Unlike most of the men, Phil had been openly fascinated by the crafting supplies, not so much by the beads and lace and adornments, but what he called spare body parts. His reaction to the doll heads was predictable as he could relate them to Dale, comparing the crocheted head to a porcelain ready-made head, complete with a smiling face and sometimes wire-rimmed glasses.

The trays of eyes and noses had sparked his interest more than anything else, probably because he'd never seen such things before. While Grace had been trying to select eyes and noses for a teddy-bear-making project for the Thursday evening ladies' craft group, Phil had picked up and commented on every nose in every bin. First, he predicted what animal would have such a nose, then he matched the nose with a completely wrong set of eyes. He'd matched bear noses to cat eyes, dog noses to doll eyes, and every combination in between. The whole time, he commented on mixing the various traits of the different animals and made up names for his new creations until he had not only her, but everyone in the area in stitches. She couldn't recall the number of times he'd made her lose count as she tried to compile faces for two-dozen animals, which the ladies' group planned to donate to a local charity for underprivileged children.

A gust of wind caused Grace to shiver as she walked, so she pulled her collar up higher. Still, the day was beautiful and slightly warmer than average for the time of year.

Phil also shivered with the wind, but instead of playing with his collar, he slapped his upper arms with his palms.

"Your idea to go skating today was a good one. It may be a little windy, but otherwise the weather is perfect."

The weather condition for skating was the last thing on Grace's mind. The weather for the moment was being very good to Phil. Unlike her, he hadn't worn a hat, and the wind gusts intermittently rippled through his hair. The winter nip turned his cheeks to an attractive rosy pink, giving him a fresh and carefree appearance. His charming little grin and carefree gait only made the whole picture of Phillip McLean more attractive.

As they walked down the block to where they'd parked the car, she noticed many women eyeing Phil in passing. Obviously he caught the interest of the general female population, because she knew no one was looking at her one-season-out-of-style coat.

Phil's voice beside her interrupted her thoughts, which was not a bad thing.

"I forgot to ask, how was Thanksgiving dinner at your parents' house? I hope you didn't have a hard time driving home. The roads were fine in the city, but you were out on the highway, where it can get gusty and slippery."

"The roads were bare in most places, and driving was good. Actually, I left a little early. Not because of the road conditions, but because I couldn't listen to my sister any longer." She stopped talking for a few steps while she collected her thoughts on the evening. "Phil, do you mind if I ask you something?"

"Not at all. Ask away."

"You're the same age as me, twenty-five, right?"

"Actually, I'm twenty-seven, but close enough. Why?"

Grace slowed her pace, forcing Phil to slow beside her so they wouldn't arrive at the car before she finished what she wanted to say. This was one topic she wanted to be over before they had to share the close quarters of his car.

She kept her focus straight forward, not looking to the left or right as she spoke. "I don't know why I'm telling you this. I don't even talk about it with my girlfriends, but that's probably because I don't want to hear it from them, too." She stopped talking for a second to try and think of how to word her question, but decided to simply blurt it out. "Does your family ever bug you about why you're not married?"

"Not really, but I can feel it coming this Christmas. My cousin Trevor is younger than me. Not only is he married, but their baby is due just after Christmas. Watching Janice walk around looking like she's got a basketball under her shirt is a kind of in-your-face reminder. With my aunt about to become a grandmother, I can only imagine that my mother is going to ask when it's going to be her turn. The concept of potential grandchildren generally does that to parents. Why do you ask? Did your mother give you a rough time on Thanksgiving?"

"She dropped a few hints, but the one who wouldn't leave me alone was my sister. You know, the one who gave me the *Name Your Baby* book?"

"Ah, yes. I don't think I'll ever forget that one."

"Pardon me?"

Grace turned her head as they continued walking, but this time Phil wouldn't turn to look at her. "Nothing," he mumbled.

"I tried to tell my mother and my sister that when God's timing is right, it will happen, but my sister just doesn't know when to quit. Usually it doesn't bother me, but this year I just couldn't listen anymore. I excused myself by saying I had to get up early for work and left shortly after supper, which was rude, and I'm not normally like that. Now I feel I should phone and apologize, but I don't want to reopen the same can of worms."

"I don't want to make excuses for them, but they probably just want you to be happy and don't realize how much it hurts to keep hounding you about it. I don't know what the solution is. Maybe there isn't one. You can't get married just to please them. You said it yourself earlier. It will happen when God decides the timing is right. I say the same thing about my own life, too."

They reached the car, saving her from having to respond. Phil unlocked the passenger door and held it open for her as she bundled the skirt of her coat around her knees and slid in. He stood behind the car until traffic eased up enough for him to open the driver's door, and soon they were on their way.

Fortunately, Phil didn't say anything more. She didn't know if he thought the conversation on the topic was finished, or if he knew she didn't want to talk about it any-more. Either way, she appreciated his silence more than words could say. However, even though she definitely was finished talking about her prospects of a future marriage, she wasn't finished thinking about it.

The main reason her sister and her mother had pushed the issue of marriage was that they were counting on their fingers the months she had been dating Neil. Over the past year she'd learned much about Neil, and he was very much the type of man she wanted to marry versus the type of man she wouldn't.

During her growing-up years, she'd always considered her father to be brave and strong, as most children did. Also, like most children, she'd never considered whether or not her parents were happy. In her teenage years, when she was starting to take interest in the interpersonal relationships of those around her, especially her family, she suddenly didn't like what she saw.

Instead of seeing her father as the strong, silent type, she started seeing his true colors as controlling and manipulative. As a child, she'd always thought her mother was merely anxious to please her father, but as she grew older, she learned the reasons why, and they weren't good, or acceptable, to Grace as an adult. Her father never actually threatened her mother with physical violence—his methods were far more subtle. He said and did things that left her mother unable to complain, yet still very much under Grace's father's thumb. The constant belittling and unfair demands, which resulted in her mother being completely under her father's control, amounted to nothing short of emotional abuse. Over the years, Grace had tried to convince her mother to attend counseling sessions, but her mother wouldn't go, claiming all was fine, when Grace knew it wasn't.

And then her sister married the same type of man as her father. Selfish, demanding, and controlling.

Grace had seen too much of that to let herself fall into the same trap. When she became a Christian, she learned of God's desire for his children to be happy and successful in their marital relationships. Therefore, when the time came for Grace to get married, she planned to marry a man who would love her in the way the Bible directed—a man who would love her in the same way that Christ loved the church, unselfishly and completely, enough that he would lay down his life for her. Of course, she expected no less of herself.

Rather than starting by weeding out the negatives, Grace wanted to seek out the positives. In Neil, she had met and developed a relationship with a man who made no demands, who valued her opinion, and always offered her free choices. His easygoing nature and flexibility made him easy to like, and she always enjoyed the time spent with him. Now, after dating each other exclusively for a year, she wondered if the time would soon come when Neil would broach the subject of marriage.

"Grace? We're home."

Her cheeks turned pink, not from the cold, but from the heat of her blush. "Oh, sorry, Phil. I was thinking about something."

"So I gathered. If you want to think about something, why don't you think about what Neil made for supper while we were gone? He said he was going to try and make something special."

Grace forced herself to smile. In the entire year, Neil had never cooked for her, and from what Phil had said about Neil's cooking, that wasn't necessarily a bad thing.

"You claim to be a better cook than Neil, and you know what he's like in the kitchen. What do you think he's doing? Just so I know what to expect."

"If we're lucky, it will be one of those hamburger casseroles that come in a box."

"And if we're not lucky?"

"I really haven't a clue. We just have to take our chances."

The scent of something cooking wafted at them when they opened the door to go in, but Grace couldn't identify what it was, other than cooking beef.

"Hey, Neil! We're back! Grace found the beads, so we had a great shopping trip."

Neil appeared in the hallway, wiping his hands on the dish towel. "That's great. Supper's not quite ready, but there's still some coffee if you want it."

Phil turned to her. "Want some? I think I'm going to have a cup. I need something to warm me up."

"Sure."

The three of them walked into the kitchen together, where Grace saw that the meal of the day was spaghetti.

She turned to Neil and smiled. "Since you're making supper, would you like me to set the table?" Grace reached up to the cupboard she suspected held the plates, but Neil raised one finger in the air and wagged it at her.

"Nope. I said I'd make supper, and that means doing everything. You guys can go into the living room, and I'll finish up."

She smiled. "I won't argue with that."

Her smile widened when Phil turned off the television and selected a CD.

"I see you have the haloless Dale still on top of the television."

Phil picked Dale up, patted the hair, then put her down again. "Yeah. I still figure it's the safest place in the house. The only reason the halo got broken was because I was fooling around with it. I figure he looks good here, don't you? Besides, in a few weeks we'll have our Christmas tree up, and he'll be moved to his place of honor, where he belongs in the first place."

"I can't believe Christmas is coming so fast. With Thanksgiving over, the Christmas stuff will be out in full force. I wonder if they're going to start playing Christmas songs at the coffeehouse. Are you sure you won't come with us?"

"Positive."

Grace waited for him to elaborate, but he didn't. Before she could ask him a second time, Neil called them into the kitchen to eat.

The spaghetti was very average, neither good nor bad, which was to be expected with canned sauce mixed with the ground beef, which was slightly overcooked, but still quite edible. Neil also served a slightly overheated garlic bread, which was okay if they cut off the outer crusts and no one ate the end pieces. Still, considering what Phil said about Neil's cooking skills, she had to give him credit for his work. More than anything, it gave her heart a thrill to know he'd cooked just for her.

They had barely finished eating when Phil reminded them that since it was only the second week the coffeehouse was running, it would be best to leave early to ensure a good table. Once again, Grace asked Phil if he was sure he wouldn't go with them, but his answer remained the same.

Seeing they had less time than expected to get there, Neil conned Phil into doing the dishes, and they left.

Somehow, the trip to the coffeehouse seemed odd, like something was missing. The something was someone, and that someone was Phil.

They were seated at a small table for two. Automatically, Grace sat so that she faced the stage. Neil sat opposite her, and they made pleasant small talk while they waited for everything to begin. To her relief, Neil didn't talk too much about the latest hockey game. Right on time, the emcee stepped onto the stage, introduced the band, and the music began.

The building was the same, the band was much the same, but Grace couldn't help but think of the difference from the previous week. This week, there was no Phil. Instead, she was with Neil, and Neil alone. In the past few weeks, she'd spent so much time with Phil or with Phil and Neil together, she'd almost forgotten what it was like to be alone with Neil.

To her surprise, at the end of the first song, Neil dragged his chair almost beside her. He positioned his chair so the two of them sat at angles at the rear of the small table, as close to side by side as was possible around a table with a top not much bigger than the size of a large pizza.

Grace thought it was the most romantic thing Neil had ever done. Unfortunately, it was probably less to sit close to her and more so that he wouldn't have his back to the band.

Neil leaned toward her and nudged her arm. "They're really good, aren't they?" he whispered barely above the volume of the music.

"Yes. Phil would really like them, too,"

Before she could close her mouth, Grace nearly choked on her words. She was on a date with Neil. The man to whom her sister said it was time to get married. She shouldn't have been thinking of Phil and how much he would be enjoying the music.

Neil leaned toward her again. "Isn't this the song Phil wanted the music for?"

She squeezed her eyes shut. "Yes, I think so."

"It's too bad he didn't come, but then this is the first time in a long time we've had the chance to be alone together on the weekend. I don't really miss him."

Neil moved his hand between the two chairs, almost like he was reaching specifically toward her.

Quickly, Grace leaned forward and wrapped both hands around her warm coffee mug.

Pointedly, she didn't respond to Neil's comment. She had to agree that it had been a long time since they'd been out alone together. But, unlike Neil, she did miss Phil, even though it had only been an hour since they parted.

Grace cleared her throat. "I wonder what Phil's doing right now? He said he had something planned for tonight. Any ideas?"

Neil also leaned forward and also wrapped his hands around his coffee mug.

"Nope," he mumbled as the music played. "I have no idea what he had planned for tonight."

Chapter 12

Phillip closed one eye and let his tongue curl out the corner of his mouth as he painstakingly positioned the microscopic bead between his fingers and poked the hairlike wire through the hole. With one more bead on the wire, he stopped to rub his sore eyes and wondered if maybe he needed glasses. He couldn't count how many beads he had dropped or how many had rolled off the kitchen table onto the floor. Since he had a whole tube for a small project, at this point Phillip had no intention of picking up the ones that had rolled away to parts unknown. He would save his eyes and simply sweep them up and give the remainder of the tube to Grace for future projects, if there were any left by the time he was finished.

Phillip stared at the small length of beads on the wire. All he was doing was making a single length. He couldn't see how people made massive artworks of beads, some of them distinct mathematical patterns or even pictures, and called it fun. He wasn't having much fun. Actually, he wasn't having any fun at all.

Once more, Phillip rubbed his eyes, then added another bead to the wire, knowing soon he was bound to reach the length he'd calculated his granny had used to make the right-sized halo. The closer he came to filling the wire, the more he couldn't believe how much time the small project was taking.

When he finally filled the required length of wire with enough beads, he pushed the beads together tightly and twisted the wire closed to form a circle with his fingers. He decidedly avoided using his needle-nosed pliers, as that was how his troubles with Dale began, this time.

Finally, he poked the base of the halo into the spot on the back of Dale's head where the original halo had been, and he was done. Immediately he returned Dale to his new home atop the television.

With Dale once more restored to normal, Phillip allowed himself to relax. He was starting to see why Granny valued the angel so much, if each step of the creative process required such painstaking effort and concentration. The starching alone, when the angel was complete, was grueling enough. Now, after making a new halo, Phillip could only imagine the work involved in the actual construction of the angel itself, if he was so exhausted after making what was probably the easiest part of the whole package.

Phillip stood back from the television, crossed his arms, and continued to study Dale from a distance. Dale was truly beautiful, of that there was no doubt. Knowing now what he didn't know before, Phillip couldn't help but wonder why women made such items when they were so much work. If it were up to him, he wasn't sure all the effort was worth it.

Yet, he knew that Grace enjoyed doing crafts, and she was good at it. Now that he knew how time-consuming such things could be, he wondered where she found the time.

The more Phillip stared at Dale, the more he thought of Grace. In fact, lately thoughts of Grace were filling inordinate amounts of his time, and he couldn't help himself. It wasn't only when Dale was involved that he thought of her either. At different points in the day, he found himself simply picturing her smile or remembering something she'd said.

And right now, she was on a date with her boyfriend, Phillip's best friend, which was how they met in the first place.

The knowledge hit him right in the solar plexus.

He didn't know when it started or how, but he had it bad.

Phillip didn't know how he'd gotten himself into such a mess, but he did know that he had to get himself out of it. Of course, the most obvious solution would be to simply not see her again, but he'd already tried that. It not only didn't work, the idea had completely backfired on him.

He didn't know how it happened, but after Neil's feeble attempt at impressing Grace with his cooking skills, they had somehow decided that once a week the three of them would have a home-cooked supper together, and they would rotate who did the cooking.

After seeing Grace on Monday for his guitar lesson, Tuesday he would be cooking her supper. Of course Neil would also be there, but at this point he didn't know which was worse, being alone with her or being forced to watch her with Neil. Either way, being with her only rubbed in his face the fact that he couldn't have her.

Then, Wednesday was Bible study night. Since he already knew many of the people present, they asked him to switch and make that one his home group. He'd been so honored to be asked that before he thought about what he was doing, he agreed. It hadn't been until afterward that he remembered the reason he had picked the other group in the first place. He and Neil had decided to attend different groups because they didn't want to see too much of each other, since they already lived together. Now, to make matters worse, not only would he be going to Bible studies with Neil, he would also be going with Grace.

Friday evenings were usually wide open. Typically, after a busy week at work, unless he had specific plans, Phillip preferred to stay home on Fridays. However, in discussion, an earlier conversation had come back to haunt him. He'd opened the door for Grace to come over to their house with Neil, regardless if he was there or not. Grace had said that, like Phillip, she welcomed the chance to relax on Friday evening and not have to make plans just because it was Friday.

Before Phillip could take her reasoning to the next step, Grace had made plans with Neil that she would come over more often on Fridays if he agreed to keep the television turned off. Then she had said with a wink toward Phillip that they would turn the music on loud. Starting, of course, the next Friday.

Phillip couldn't protest without having to explain why, so therefore he forced a smile and agreed.

For the next month, Grace had a list of activities she wanted to do on Saturdays as a group, all with himself and Neil, and even a couple including her friend June. At the top of the list were skating and more trips to the Christian coffeehouse.

And then Sunday there was church, where they attended together.

Fortunately, Thursday was Grace's ladies' group craft meetings, where no man dared to go.

Thursdays, he would be safe.

"Phil? What are you doing here?"

The sounds of snipping and the rustle of fabric faded

into silence as all the ladies in the room stopped their projects and turned to look at him, the only male in the room.

Phillip felt the heat of his blush spread from his neck all the way to the tips of his ears. From the back of the room, his granny waved at him, so he waved back while he waited for Grace, who had left her table and approached him.

He dropped his voice to a whisper so no one could hear, especially his granny. "Sorry to interrupt, Grace. I have to talk to you. It's important. It's Dale."

Before she could respond, Phil wrapped his fingers around her arm and gently led her from the room and into the hall so he could talk more freely.

"What happened? I thought Dale was safe on top of the television."

"I thought so, too, but I was wrong. Neil's brother came over tonight to watch the hockey game with Neil, and he brought his kids. Neil's brother started teasing him about Dale being on top of the television while the game was on, and without telling me, they put Dale on the coffee table."

Grace visibly shuddered. "No... Not more coffee."

Phillip shook his head. "Worse. Neil's nephews started playing with it. And one of them got gum in it."

"Oh, no!" Grace's hands flew to her cheeks, which Phillip would have thought quite cute if it wasn't for the gnawing in the pit of his stomach at the latest accident. "Gum is one of the hardest things to get out. Sometimes impossible!"

"I know. That's why I came now. I feel sick thinking about it. Maybe if we tackle it right away, we can get it out."

"What does Neil have to say about this?"

"He feels significantly guilty, but that doesn't do me any good. All I want is for Dale to be clean and back to normal. Help me, Grace. I don't know what to do."

"Where's Dale now?"

"In the car."

"Okay, that's good. You were right to want to start working on it immediately. This way we'll have the best chance of success. I know my book has a part on removing gum, so we can do it at my place. Oh, by the way, I hope you don't mind giving me a ride. I came with Elsie. I just have to go back in and pack up my stuff and tell her I'm not coming back." She stopped talking, scrunched her brows for a second, then she broke out into a wide smile. Phillip found himself fascinated, watching the interplay of expression. He could almost see the lightbulb going on in her head.

Grace raised one finger in the air. "I just got a great idea! I can tell everyone you're here to give me a ride home, and you accidentally came early, so your granny won't wonder why you came. You are giving me a ride, so it is the truth."

"Great idea. I'll go wait in the car."

At Grace's nod, Phillip walked outside, but he didn't open the car door. He knew he wouldn't be able to sit still. Once in the car, he would have nothing to amuse himself except for looking at poor Dale with the lump of gum stuck to his wing. However, what lay ahead would be worse.

While they fixed Dale, he and Grace would be alone.

He wasn't sure that was advisable, but with Dale on the line, he had no alternative.

As expected, he hadn't been able to avoid spending time with Grace for the past week. In fact, he'd seen her every single day since he made his decision not to see so much of her. If he had to see a bright side, he'd been successful at keeping himself focused and at a safe distance because Neil had always been there. He'd even endured Neil's teasing about his bad guitar playing because Neil's presence kept his time with Grace centered on only the guitar lesson and not on personal issues. Tuesday Phillip had made supper, but he'd stayed in the kitchen while Neil and Grace remained in the living room. He'd tried not to be interested in what they were doing, but it still came as a great relief to hear Neil flipping channels looking for a show he never did find. He'd found it highly amusing to listen as Grace complained more and more every time Neil hit the button for the next channel.

Wednesday night had been one of the rare times Neil didn't have to work late. Therefore, they had attended the Bible study meeting as a threesome. Since most of the attendees were their age and single, he had been able to separate himself while they were allegedly together.

But tonight, soon Grace would emerge from the church basement, alone. She would get into the car with him. They would go to her apartment. For the rest of the evening, it would be just the two of them.

Phillip blew a puff of breath into the cold, evening air and watched the cloud slowly dissipate. The only thing between himself and Grace tonight would be Dale. For the moment, he didn't need a Christmas angel to broadcast glad tidings. He needed a guardian angel to keep his heart safe.

The church door creaked open and banged shut. Grace's footsteps crunched in the snow as she cut across the grounds, taking the shortest way instead of keeping to the sidewalk.

"I'm here. Where is she?"

With shaking hands, Phillip finally opened the car door and pulled Dale out from behind his seat. Once he handed Dale to Grace, he pushed the car door closed to keep the heat inside.

Grace shifted slightly to catch the light from the streetlight, then she turned Dale over and poked at the blob with one finger. "This isn't too bad; it's only one small spot. I had pictured strings of gum all over her."

"I know you're trying to make me feel better, but I suppose it could be worse. Do you think we can get it out?"

"It's only the size of a quarter. I don't see why not. Even if a little dark spot remains, it's at the back where no one would see it once Dale is on top of the tree. But we can certainly try to get the whole thing out. My book has instructions for everything. I'm sure it will say how to get gum out. Between the two of us, I know we can do it." Abruptly, she lowered Dale and dropped her voice to a whisper. "We had better get going. I don't want any of the ladies, especially your granny, to see what we've got. If the reason you came was just to give me a ride, pretty soon they're going to be wondering what we're doing still standing here."

"You're right." Phillip turned his head to watch the church basement window to see if there were any faces peeking through at the same time as he reached toward the car door to open it for Grace. Instead of the cold metal of the handle, his fingers rested on warm skin.

Unable to stop himself, Phillip wrapped his fingers around Grace's hand and gave it a gentle squeeze. "I was going to do that for you."

Phillip knew he was going to regret it, but he couldn't stop himself. He closed his fingers around Grace's delicate hand and rubbed his thumb into her wrist as he gently pulled her hand off the door handle. Not releasing her hand, he reached over with his free hand and opened the door for her.

He smiled, gave her hand one more gentle squeeze, and let go when he had the door open all the way. "M'Lady," he said as he closed his eyes for a second and bowed his head slightly as a signal for her to slide into the car. "Your chariot awaits."

At first she didn't move, and then she was in the car so quickly he barely had time to blink before she pulled the door closed.

Phillip walked around the car, slid in behind the wheel, and they were on their way.

"So what was everybody doing today? Were you using all those eyes and noses you bought on the weekend?"

Grace stared out the window, not looking at him as she spoke. "Yes. Everyone is making one bear, and we're going to donate them all to a children's charity the weekend after next."

"I'm sorry to interrupt you. I know you enjoy making stuff like that, plus it's for a worthy cause."

"It's okay. We were just cutting the bears out and putting on the eyes and noses. We all have to take the pieces home anyway to sew them together. Next week we're going to stuff them."

Grace rambled on about making bears and other stuffed toys for the remainder of the drive to her apartment. Phillip didn't mind. In fact, he was glad to have her stare out the window, talking nonstop and refusing to look at him. That meant she couldn't see the smile that he couldn't wipe off his face.

He'd rattled her. That said a lot, because he was rattled, too. Ever since the first time Dale needed to be fixed and he'd run over to her apartment, something about Grace affected him like no woman before her. He'd never experienced anything like the instant bond that continued to grow like an out-of-control forest fire with every passing day. The bond was such that he didn't even have to be specifically with her or talk to her to feel it. Just knowing she was in the same room or the same building, knowing he could go find her at any moment, gave him peace and comfort at the same time as an inner excitement. The emotions shouldn't have mixed, but they did. When they were actually together, side by side, the rush he felt was even more intense. Being with Grace made his mind race and his heart pound. Her smile made him think all things were possible, just because she believed in him.

And now he knew that he wasn't the only one affected.

Phillip could no longer deny it. He had fallen in love with his best friend's girlfriend.

However, Phillip couldn't tell what was going on between Neil and Grace. Nor did he know exactly how she felt about him, only that he had somehow disquieted her today, along with himself. Whatever had just passed between them confirmed that whatever was happening had crossed some kind of line he couldn't quite define.

But, there was a catch, and it was a huge one. Grace's relationship with Neil could not be ignored. Phillip had talked to Grace enough to know that she was ready to settle down. Whether that would be with Neil still remained to be seen.

Phillip wished he could find out the level of commitment on both sides of that relationship. Then, once he knew, he would make a choice. Even though it would be the hardest thing he ever would have to do in his life, if it was God's will for Grace to be with Neil, he would step back. But if God wanted Phillip to be Grace's life partner, that would make him the happiest man on Earth.

Phillip had never been good at waiting, God's timing or not. Most often he became impatient and took matters into his own hands and made things happen. In this case, even though it felt like it could kill him, he couldn't take the chance. This time he had to sit back and wait for God's direction or some sign indicating what he should do, whether or not it was what he wanted to happen. The only thing he knew for sure was he would be spending a lot of time in prayer. Either that or go insane.

As he parked the car in the visitor parking area, Grace

fished her keys out of her purse. "I think we've got a better chance at getting this gum out because it hasn't dried yet. I'll take our injured angel, and you take that bag of bear parts, and let's get moving. We can't waste any time because it's starting to dry out already."

Phillip nodded and followed Grace inside.

Chapter 13

Grace paged through the book, trying to ignore Phil's breath on her cheek as he read over her shoulder, even though his presence sent tingles up and down her spine.

She rested her finger on the page. "It says to rub ice on the gum to harden it, then chip it away with a dull knife. After that, dab with grease solvent, then launder with regular detergent. What's grease solvent?"

"That's what you use to clean your hands after working on the motor in the car or fixing the lawn mower. I've got some in the garage. But I can't see putting that on Dale. It stinks. I would think that the solvent is oil based, too, because it leaves a stain on the rags."

Grace closed the book, stepped forward, and turned around, more so to put some distance between herself and Phil than needing to look at him as she spoke. "That would be why it says to wash it after you use the solvent, to prevent a stain after the gum is gone. I have an idea. Why don't you go home and get the solvent, and I'll start right away with the ice part. I don't want to delay any longer, in case it sets or something. I've never had to take gum out of anything before; I only heard that it's hard."

"That makes sense." Phil checked his watch. "It's probably quicker to go home and get the can out of the garage than go to the store and buy some new stuff. I'll be back as quick as I can."

He didn't wait for her to see him to the door, but let himself out.

All was silent as Grace stared at the door, the book still in her hands.

She didn't know what was happening, but it had to stop.

Grace didn't want her knees to shake or her throat to go dry whenever Phil came close to her. She didn't want to tremble at his touch, especially when it was accidental, and he didn't necessarily mean anything by it. At the car, his brief, but gentle ministrations set her quivering all over. His touch felt like the touch of a lover, gentle and soothing, yet at the same time giving the hint of more. Grace knew that Phil hadn't meant it that way. They were friends, nothing more.

She couldn't deny that in the short space of time since they'd really started seeing each other, either despite Neil's presence or maybe even because of it, she and Phil had grown quite close. They could talk about anything, and they understood each other. Phil was fun to be with. He made her laugh, and she knew she made him laugh.

Even Tiger liked him.

Grace thumped the book on the table. She didn't want to think about Phil. The reason she was home and not still at craft night was to work on Dale.

Quickly, she removed two ice cubes from the freezer, fetched a couple of washcloths with which to hold the ice so she wouldn't freeze her fingers, then she set to work rubbing the ice on the gum. By the time Phil returned, she'd managed to chip some of the gum away, but not all.

"How's it going?"

Grace laid the ice and washcloths on the table and held Dale up for Phil to see, welcoming the break. The washcloths had protected her fingers somewhat from the chill of the ice, but not completely.

"It's going pretty good, but not as fast as I hoped."

"How are your hands? If your fingers are getting a little numb from holding that ice so long, I can take a turn. After all, it's my problem, really."

"I'm not going to argue with that."

Phil dragged the other chair so they angled together, then sat so they were knee-to-knee at about a forty-five-degree angle. He took Dale from her and set to work with the ice.While Phil rubbed at the gum with an ice cube on each side of the wing, Grace blew on her hands, then crossed her arms and tucked her fingers under her armpits to get some feeling and her circulation back.

"You know what I was thinking? Maybe you should put Dale in a box in the closet until you actually set up your tree. Your living room doesn't seem to be a very safe place."

Phil rested one of the cloth-covered ice cubes on the table, shook his fingers in the air, blew on them, picked at the lump with the knife, then resumed his task with the ice. "It's not my living room that's doing it. This all has been centering around the television. I only have to get Dale away from the television, and I think we'll be fine."

"Maybe it's not the television; it's all the hockey that seems to always be on."

Phil's rhythm faltered for just a second. "You know, Neil is much better company before hockey season."

Grace stared at Phil, waiting for him to elaborate, but

he didn't, nor did he raise his head. He merely continued to rub the ice on the gum.

"Neil told me there are two games on Saturday, a doubleheader. I think he wants to stay home and watch both of them, back-to-back. I don't mind hockey, but I'm really not interested enough to sit and watch two whole games."

"I know what you mean. I like hockey, and I can't sit for two whole games. At least not until the play-offs. I think I got off the last hunk of gum possible. Do you think it's time to try the solvent on the rest?"

Grace blinked to let her mind catch up to his quick change of subjects. She leaned toward Phil and touched the spot while he held Dale out. Some gum still remained stuck to the threads, but she knew they'd never be able to scrape off every single bit. "I guess that's as good as we're going to get. The instructions don't say at what point to give up on the ice and go on to the next step. It doesn't look like we're going to be able to get any more off with the ice. How do you use solvent?"

"I just pour it on my hands and wipe it off with a rag, and the grease comes off onto the rag. I don't know how much we should rub Dale; after all, he's only made of thread." Phil opened the cap and was about to pour some directly on the spot, but Grace raised one palm in the air to stop him.

"Just a minute. I'll go get a cloth from under the sink. The instructions in the book said to dab it with the solvent. I think that means to pour some on a cloth and work it from there, not to pour it directly on the gum."

"Yeah. I guess it's better to be safe than sorry."

Grace soaked a piece of a cloth with the solvent, then began the process of gently dabbing the spot. "It's working! Praise the Lord!"

Phil's relief was almost tangible as he sagged in the

chair. In silence, she continued to dab at the remainder until all of the gum residue really did come off.

"Now let's get her into the sink to wash off the solvent. Then all we'll have to do is starch her again."

Phil let out an exaggerated groan, at which Grace couldn't help but smile. "Stop it. You know this is good news."

They stood simultaneously, but with the placement of the chairs, neither could move away. They stood face-to-face, inches apart, with only the bedraggled Dale between them.

Phil's hands rose and drifted up until he cupped her cheeks with his palms. His voice came out low-pitched and rough, not like Phil at all. "Thank you, Grace. I don't know what to say. I know this sounds corny, but you're wonderful. I really mean that."

Very slowly, Grace felt Phil's rough thumbs gently pressing into her cheeks. The soft pressure of his touch electrified her. She knew she should have moved away, but she couldn't. All she could do was look up at him, into his fascinating eyes. The color had darkened to almost a dark gray, all traces of the green were gone.

Just like another time that burned into her memory, she thought he was going to kiss her. Only this time, she had no doubt about what she wanted to happen. This time, she did want him to kiss her.

She could barely discern the difference, but the pressure of Phil's hands against her chin shifted ever so slightly, tipping her face just a little more up to his.

Grace backed away so fast she bumped the chair with the backs of her knees, sending it askew. She rested one palm on the table to her left, barely able to still hold Dale with her right. Phil's hands fell to his sides.

"You fill the kitchen sink with warm water and I'll get some laundry detergent. No, wait. I still have dishes in the sink. I ran off so fast tonight, I didn't do the dishes first. I'm so embarrassed. Here, you hold Dale."

Not giving Phil an opportunity to protest, Grace thrust Dale at him, giving him only a second to grasp Dale before he would risk dropping the angel. In one continuous motion, Grace turned around and reached the sink in three strides. She piled the dirty dishes on the counter, wiped out the sink, and then filled it with warm water. She squatted down and reached into the cupboard for the box of detergent and stood. "You can bring Dale now; I'm ready for her."

Phil shuffled to her side, slowly lowering Dale into the warm water. Instead of stepping back, he turned toward her.

Grace kept her attention focused fully on Dale, beneath the surface of the water.

"I'm sorry, Grace. Please, don't be upset. I promise that will never happen again. I was out of line."

"It's okay," she mumbled, not moving her head. She couldn't look at Phil now. She didn't want to see his eyes, the eyes that would make her change her mind about what was happening in her heart. "Let's just forget about it and get this done. Pretty soon we'll have Dale back to normal again. You know where the starch is by now. Would you like to get it out? Use two of those scoops, and you can start heating it up so we can finish tonight."

"Okay."

Without asking for help, Phil measured the right amount of starch into the pot, then went into the bathroom to add the water rather than get in her way while she washed Dale in the kitchen sink. Also without asking, he immediately began to heat it up on the stove, stirring while it heated, just as he'd seen her do the other times she'd made the starch mixture.

"How do I know when it's ready?"

Grace held Dale up out of the water and held the wing section up to the light, trying to determine if all the solvent residue had come out. "See how it's kind of cloudy? When it goes clear, then it's done. It has to boil for a couple of minutes. You'll be able to see the difference when it happens."

"Okay."

The sight of Phil bending over and looking into the pot, trying to analyze the color and consistency of the starch mixture as it approached the boiling point, stopped her in her tracks.

Grace had seldom seen a man standing over the stove, but, while Phil did look out of place, he appeared comfortable as he stirred, then held the spoon up, and watched the thickening liquid drip back into the pot.

She cleared her throat. "Since you're having so much fun making that, did you know that if you didn't put in so much cornstarch and put in some lemon juice and sugar with that, you could make lemon sauce for Chinese Lemon Chicken?"

He grinned, setting off those charming laugh lines at the corners of his fascinating eyes. "Really? That's neat. I love Lemon Chicken. If this is all there is to it, I can do that. Wouldn't Neil be surprised? Although he wouldn't believe me that I made it myself. Do you have a recipe? Can you show me how to do the chicken, too?"

"Sure."

The word barely spoken, Grace snapped her mouth shut. After what nearly happened only a few minutes ago, she couldn't believe that she'd just offered to give him a cooking lesson, another time where she would be alone with him.

Not that she didn't trust Phil; she trusted him more than she'd ever trusted anyone in her life.

It was herself she didn't trust.

"That's great! How about Saturday, while Neil is watching the hockey games? Just tell me what to buy, and I'll have it ready. All we have to do is stick our heads around the corner to cheer appropriately a few times, and then he won't miss either one of us. And just think of the great supper we'll have, although that means I get an extra cooking night. Wait a minute. I don't know if that's fair."

His grin widened. Grace couldn't think to reply.

Phil leaned down to investigate the starch mixture. "I think it's thick enough, and I see what you mean about it going clear. If I put my coat and boots and stuff back on and went outside on the balcony and stirred it outside, do you think it will cool faster, so we can dunk Dale in it sooner? Even if all I do is put the pot in the snow, that will cool it down somewhat."

"Good idea. Let's do that."

Phil donned his outdoor clothing and disappeared through the balcony door while Grace wrung Dale out and blotted out as much excess moisture as she could with a bath towel.

As she pressed Dale with the towel, out of the corner of her eye she watched Phil through the sliding-glass door leading to the balcony. Almost as if he didn't have a care in the world, he moved the pot to different places in the snow, stirred, then moved the pot again as the heat melted the snow. With every move, the snow melted less and less quickly, and he moved the pot more and more slowly.

After awhile, she couldn't stand it. Grace pulled on her coat and boots and joined him.

"You look like you're having so much fun out here. How's it coming?"

She reached down to stir the mixture and test it herself, but stopped with her hand hovering in the air. "You made a picture of a Christmas tree with the pot."

"Yeah, and I almost finished, too. I just have to touch

up the one side, but the pot isn't warm enough to melt the snow anymore."

Grace sighed, pretending to be annoyed rather than admit how his playfulness charmed her. "This just proves that men are little boys who got tall."

The grin never left his face. "So what's your point?"

Grace giggled as they poked holes in the snow in the indents that comprised the Christmas tree, making ornaments. Together they piled snow on the top of the tree to mold it into the best image of Dale they could, before they went inside.

The starching process progressed quicker this time than the last time, no doubt learned from repetition. They finished just before midnight. Even though it was late and they were both obviously tired, knowing that Dale was fixed once more and all would be fine filled Grace with a tremendous amount of satisfaction. Despite all the work, Grace simply enjoyed her evening with Phil. She'd had fun, and she knew he had, too, even though they both had been fighting back yawns for the past hour.

After everything was packed up and Dale was once more in place, supported by the network of books and chopsticks to hold her up over the heat vent while she dried, Phil put his coat back on for the third time that evening. On the way to the door, he became more and more quiet and increasingly somber.

Grace opened the door and stepped out into the hall, but Phil didn't follow.

He spoke so quietly she could barely hear him. "Grace, I don't want to sound like your sister, but I have to ask. Why is it that you're not married?"

Visions of the two marriages closest to her flashed through her mind. Grace loved her father as any daughter would, but seeing her parents' relationship from an adult perspective, her mother was trapped in a marriage to a man who demanded much and gave so little, as was her sister. Grace had decided long ago that she would not follow the pattern of her family. Both her mother and her sister had married too young, without having achieved enough experience or maturity to make an intelligent decision on the most important choice a person would ever make.

Grace was in no rush to get married. Over and over she told herself that she would not make the same mistake. God desired a marriage to last a lifetime, and she wanted hers to be under God's blessings and God's guidelines for her marriage, along with every other aspect of her life. When God gave her the right man, and after enough time passed when she knew he would not dominate her as she'd seen her father and her brother-in-law do to her mother and her sister, only then would she consider marriage. When God showed her without a shadow of a doubt that He'd picked the right man for her.

"I don't know," she mumbled. "I guess the right man hasn't asked me."

"Oh," he muttered, then cleared his throat. "Good night, Grace."

He turned and walked to the elevator, pushed the button, and waited. Just as the elevator door opened, it occurred to Grace that she hadn't confirmed their plans for Friday night. Phil had already stepped into the elevator, so she ran down the hall, hoping to catch him.

The door was almost closed by the time she got there, with only a crack of light showing. Grace aimed her finger at the button and started to move toward it, but as the door clicked closed, she heard Phil muttering from inside, saying what sounded like him calling Neil an idiot.

She never did hit the button, but remained frozen in one spot, one finger poised in midair, as the elevator began its descent.

Grace returned to her apartment, more tired than she'd been in years, but somehow she knew it was going to be a long night.

Chapter 14

Phillip held the earring box up to his ear. "What do you think?"

Neil shook his head. "Not your color."

Grace poked Neil in the arm. "Stop it, Neil." She turned to Phillip. "I think your mom will love them. She loves purple."

Phillip held up another box. "Or maybe these? These are plain gold, so they'll go with anything."

Neil smirked and crossed his arms. "You know, Phil, I can't believe you haven't finished your Christmas shopping yet."

"What are you talking about? There's still over two weeks until Christmas. I've got lots of time. Besides, I plan to finish the rest of my shopping today. I'd like to know how you did your shopping so quickly. You hate shopping worse than I do."

Neil grinned. "I did all my shopping online or by phone this year. In one day. What I didn't have shipped direct is getting delivered to my door, in plenty of time for Christmas."

"That might work for your brothers and your friends, but what about your mom?"

"I got her a one-year membership for those Heartsong books that Grace reads all the time. Grace really likes them, so I thought my mom would, too."

"I think my mom already gets them. I better stick with the earrings. What about you, Grace? Are you all done with your shopping?"

She shook her head. "No, but I just have to get something for the drawing at work. I got the bank manager, and I really don't know what to buy him that costs under five dollars. That's the limit we set."

Neil pointed down the mall. "While Phil pays for the earrings, why don't we go down to the dollar store? They've got lots of cheap novelty stuff."

"Great idea. I also have to get stuff for my Sunday school class. Phil, want to meet us there? You're going to be in line a long time from the looks of things."

Phillip glanced briefly to the lineup, guessing eight people would be ahead of him. "Sounds good to me."

He watched Neil and Grace walk down the aisle and quickly become lost in the crowd.

They weren't holding hands. If he were with Grace in a crowded mall, and if he were dating her, he would be holding her hand. Actually, even if the mall wasn't crowded, Phillip would still be holding her hand.

A year ago, when he didn't know Grace, he hadn't understood the relationship between Neil and Grace. Now that he knew her, he understood it even less. In many ways, Phillip thought he knew Grace better than Neil did. He knew her hopes of going to night school and working her way up into a supervisory position at the bank. He knew her dreams of her ministry at the church, both through her

Sunday school class and the ever-growing ladies' ministry that was now reaching out to their community. They'd prayed together for the salvation of her family. She'd even shed a few tears and shared a number of the heartaches and frustrations in her life. In the same way, Phillip had told Grace things he'd never even told Neil, his best friend since childhood.

Phillip knew all Grace was waiting for was the right man to ask for her hand in marriage.

Neil didn't know what he had in the palm of his hand.

If he'd been holding her hand...

Which he wasn't.

By the time Phillip paid for his mother's Christmas gift, Grace and Neil were already on their way back from the dollar store, and they met halfway in the mall. Phillip picked up one more gift for his family's gift exchange to complete his Christmas shopping, and they were done.

Unlike any other Saturday for the past couple of months, tonight Grace had plans to go out to dinner with her co-workers, making this the first time in over a month that Phillip wouldn't be with her on Saturday night. Even though they'd spent the entire day together, already Phillip felt the loss.

Since their shopping was done and Grace was going out for dinner, they dropped her off in front of her apartment. If it were Phillip driving, he would have parked his car and walked her inside. But, since Neil was driving and didn't see an open spot in the visitor parking, rather than parking down the block, Neil waited in the drop-off zone by the curb until Grace unlocked the main door. The moment the door closed behind her, he drove off.

"Guess it's just you and me, tonight, my man," Neil said as he pulled into traffic.

"Yeah," Phillip muttered, staring blankly out the window. "You and me and the hockey game."

Neil grinned from ear to ear. "Just like old times. The Kings are playing the Canucks tonight. It's going to be a great game."

Phillip didn't say much while Neil quoted game stats and caught him up on everything he missed in the past month, when Phillip had spent every day with Grace instead of sitting in front of the television with Neil.

With the game starting in ten minutes, Neil parked himself on the couch as soon as they arrived home to wait through the pregame comments and the national anthems.

Finally, Phillip couldn't stand it anymore. He sat on the other couch and crossed his arms over his chest. "Look at yourself, Neil. I know Grace isn't here tonight, but you do the same thing if she's here or not. Is this the way you're going to be when you're married, with your face buried in the television all the time?"

"Married?"

Phillip dragged his hand over his face, then cleared his throat. "Neil, you've been dating Grace for the past year. Neither of you see anyone else. Don't you think that when a relationship goes that way, what you're heading for is marriage?"

"I never thought about getting married. I'm fine the way things are."

Phillip's stomach tightened. Neil may have been fine with the way things were, but he shouldn't have been. Neil should have been eager to spend time with Grace and build the relationship—eager to do things for her and looking toward the future, especially at their age. Instead, it had been Phillip who spent time with Grace every day. Many times Neil had opportunity to see Grace but had chosen to go do his own thing without her. Quite frankly, Phillip couldn't understand it.

Phillip swept one hand through the air to encompass their messy living room. "Is this the way you want to live for the rest of your life? Haven't you ever thought about settling down? A wife? Kids? Wouldn't you like to give your life some meaning?"

"Meaning?" Neil's blank stare told Phillip what Neil thought about his question.

Phillip sighed. "Look at us. We're twenty-seven, and she's twenty-five. Lots of people we know are not only married, but many of them have kids. To be honest with you, I've even been thinking of marriage lately."

Neil stared at him blankly, without comment.

Phillip waved his hand through the air, swiped his fingers through his hair, then he began to wipe his palms up and down on his pant legs. "Women usually think about that kind of thing before us guys do, but that doesn't mean it's wrong or too soon."

"What are you trying to say?"

Phillip paused to calm himself, trying to keep from shouting. "If you're not thinking that marriage is a possibility, what about Grace?"

"What about her?"

It almost hurt Phillip to say it, but he had to. "You know. You and Grace. Together. Married."

Neil shrugged his shoulders. "She's mentioned marriage a couple of times, but only because someone from church was getting married. You know. Showers and stuff like that. Women like to talk about those things. It doesn't mean anything. Besides, I know that Grace isn't interested in marriage."

"But I think she is. Hasn't she dropped little hints to you? Commented on engagement rings when you're out shopping? Or talked about other people you know who are getting married, then waited for you to say something?"

Phillip had both seen and experienced women dropping such hints, none of which Grace had done with him, but that was because his relationship with Grace was different. They had done the opposite, based on friendship only, and had talked about marriage directly. She'd come right out and said that the right man hadn't asked her, but she was only waiting for it to happen.

"Grace doesn't do stuff like that. If she wanted to get married someday, she'd tell me. Besides, I don't think we're ready for that."

All Phillip could do was stare at his best friend. "Maybe not now, but don't you think that one day, someday in the future, you might want to get married?"

Neil shrugged his shoulders. "I don't know. I've never thought about it."

The twist in Phillip's stomach turned into a full-fledged knot. Unlike Neil, he had been thinking of marriage, and not just a generic concept of married life. Lately, he'd been thinking of what it would be like to be married to Grace.

"Don't you think after all this time, you'd be feeling one way or the other about marrying Grace? If you don't see marriage as a possibility, then why have you been going out with her for so long?"

"I like her, if that's what you want to hear. We have fun together, yet we can both do our own thing when we want to. She takes me as I am, and I take her as she is."

"And that's it? That's good enough for you?"

"It works for both of us. Now be quiet. It's the opening face-off."

Phillip stood. "I don't think I'm going to watch the game. I'm going to go into my room and practice my guitar."

"Have fun. Oh! Take it! Take it! Check him! Hey, that's icing! Where's the ref?"

Phillip walked away, leaving Neil to argue all he wanted with the television.

He picked up the guitar and strummed a few chords before pulling out the lesson book, but he couldn't concentrate on the lesson. Instead of thinking about the chords and patterns he was supposed to be learning, he thought about his guitar teacher.

Grace.

He was fully and completely in love with Grace, but Grace didn't love him. She should have been in love with Neil, but quite honestly, Phillip couldn't tell how she felt about Neil. He didn't see the excitement or the driving need that he felt toward her in Grace's interactions with Neil. He certainly didn't see it in Neil. After talking to Neil, he highly doubted that Neil was in love with Grace, especially not the way Phillip was. And that hurt. Grace deserved better. She deserved to be cherished and loved and treated like the special person he knew she was.

The phone rang, giving Phillip the distraction he needed. When he picked it up, he heard Grace's voice with the noise and blare of a crowd in the background.

"Phil, I need your help. I didn't know that I parked in a no-parking zone, and they towed my car away. I'm stranded. A couple of the people from work I was meeting got sick and didn't come, so those of us who did show up had a quick burger and everyone decided to finish their Christmas shopping and reschedule the dinner for next weekend. Since I didn't have any more shopping to do, I went straight to where I parked my car to find it got towed away. Are you busy? I know Neil is watching a hockey game. Can you come and get me? I'm at the mall, at the west entrance."

For all the times Grace had dropped everything to help him, Phillip felt ecstatic that now he could finally return the favor, although the circumstances were less than happy for her. He leaned his guitar against the wall as he spoke. "I'll be right there."

He made it to the mall in ten minutes and found Grace exactly where she said she would be.

"Can we get it now?"

"No. I already phoned and they're closed for people who want to retrieve their cars, but they're gladly towing more cars there. I'm so upset! I didn't know this was a staff-only area! The only sign posted was up high on the building wall, not even in the spot I was in. I'm going to fight it, but I have to pay the money to get my car back."

"Can you get it tomorrow?"

"Yes. After church. Do you guys mind picking me up for church? I obviously need a ride."

"Not at all. You know, while we're out, Neil and I haven't bought a tree yet. Since he's otherwise occupied, how would you like to pick out a tree tonight? We were going to do it tomorrow, but there's no time like the present. Unless you have something else to do."

Her whole face lit up, telling Phillip he had made the right decision to ask her.

"Yes! I've never bought a real tree. We always had a fake tree when I was a kid, and living alone in an apartment, I only have one of those fake two-foot trees. This is going to be fun! Do you want help decorating?"

Phillip could only imagine Neil trying to watch the game around the fuss while he and Grace set up the tree and organized the decorations.

He grinned. "Yeah."

"I have friends who string popcorn and use that for garland, and it's really pretty. I guess you guys don't do that."

"Nope."

"Do you want to try it?"

This time, Phillip didn't want to think of Neil. He only thought of sitting in the kitchen with Grace over a fresh cup of coffee. He imagined the scent of the fresh pine tree filling them with the excitement of Christmas while they shared a fun time stringing popcorn with a needle and thread—which had to be much easier than stringing beads on a wire.

He grinned wider. "Yeah."

"Do you think Neil will mind being interrupted from the hockey game?"

Phillip grinned the widest yet. "Yeah."

They purchased a tree from the vendor in the corner of the mall parking lot, tied it to the roof, and giggled the entire way to Phillip's house.

Phillip struggled to turn the doorknob, then nudged the door open with his backside as they dragged the tree into the house, leaving a trail of needles behind them.

"What in the world are you two doing? Hi, Grace."

Phillip dragged the tree between the couch where Neil sat and the television on purpose. "What does it look like we're doing?"

"Okay, okay. Redundant question. Why now?"

"Why not now? We should have had the tree up last week, but we didn't have time. This is as good a time as any."

Neil sighed and shuffled to the other end of the couch. "Let me know when you're ready for my help."

Phillip pulled their box of meager decorations from the closet and set it beside the television; then he lifted the tree, and Grace wiggled underneath to tighten the bolts on the stand to support it. Together they worked on getting it straight, asking Neil if it was right every time they made a minor adjustment.

After they watered the tree, they retired to the kitchen to make the popcorn garland. That made Neil very happy, as the game was tied in only the second period.

Phillip found the sewing kit while Grace made the popcorn. He had both needles threaded at the same time the popcorn was popped and ready to string.

"I'm almost surprised you guys have a sewing kit. I was prepared to go home to bring over my own sewing kit."

Phillip poked the needle through the first popped kernel. "Hey. I'm perfectly capable of sewing on a button, and sometimes I have to, although I know some guys who take that kind of stuff home to their mothers or even pay a dry cleaner to sew on a button. That's such a waste of money. Actually, I know someone who once bought a new shirt because he lost a button."

"That's ridiculous," Grace mumbled as she began stringing popcorn as well.

"You know, this is so much easier than doing those beads. I thought I was going to go blind. I don't understand how women do that kind of thing and call it relaxing. By the way, remind me to give you the rest of the beads I didn't use. I don't ever want to look at those things again for the rest of my life."

"Pardon me?"

"Doing the popcorn is easy, but stringing the beads was really hard. They were so small, I kept dropping them."

"Dropping them? You're supposed to just let them lay on the table and steady the beads against your finger, then poke the wire through. It's actually very fast."

Phillip didn't dare reply.

"Oh, Phil… You didn't pick up every bead and do it like threading a needle each time, did you?"

Phillip concentrated intently on the piece of popcorn in his hand. "I'm not going to answer that on the grounds of incrimination."

Grace tried to stifle a giggle, not very successfully.

"Never mind. Now let's change the subject."

Just like every other time they were together, Phillip thoroughly enjoyed himself, whether they talked or shared moments or even minutes of silence.

The only part of the evening he didn't enjoy was hearing

the drone of the hockey game and Neil calling out to the television in the background. It was a reminder not only of Neil's presence, but also that he was the third wheel in their relationship. A month ago, Phillip was content to be there, but not any longer. Things had changed, but he didn't know what to do about it, which only added to his frustration.

"Done!" Grace held up her string.

Phillip tied off his shorter string and bit off the end that didn't have any popcorn on it. "I'm done, too!"

"Cheater."

"No comment."

Together they marched into the living room with the strings. As he walked between Neil and the television on their way to the tree, Phillip purposely walked slower. Neil stopped commenting on the game and craned his neck to see around them as they passed.

They continued to talk as they wrapped the garland around the tree. When they failed to get more than a grunt of response from Neil, they gave up, lowered their voices, and talked only between the two of them.

Phillip couldn't help but be annoyed at Neil. As far as Phillip was concerned, Neil shouldn't have been watching the hockey game; he should have been keeping company with his girlfriend, whom he had not been spending enough time with lately.

Phillip didn't want to come right out and ask Neil to turn off the game and join them. He wanted Neil to take the initiative himself. Therefore, to give Neil the hint, Phillip made sure that every time he walked around the tree, he moved between Neil and the game.

When the garland was arranged to perfection, Phillip opened the box of ornaments, not moving it from beside the television. In order to get Neil's attention, every time

Phillip reached into the box, he stood partway blocking the television.

Neil's face tightened, but he said nothing.

Satisfied that he was finally getting a reaction and wanting Neil to turn the game off and join them without being asked, Phillip removed two ornaments from the box and stood directly in front of the television. "Hey, Neil. What do you think? Should we put the red one or the blue one up on this long branch?"

"I don't care," Neil grumbled as he once more shuffled positions on the couch. "Will you get out of my way?"

"Oops," Phillip said, perfectly aware of what he was doing.

He handed both ornaments to Grace, then returned to the box, where he bent over so half of him blocked the screen as he selected the next ones to give to Grace. Over and over, each time he brought another decoration out of the box, he purposely blocked part of the screen from Neil's line of vision. Neil's frustration continued to build until it became a challenge for Phillip to see how much Neil would take.

Finally, at the end of the third period, the game was tied at four each, one team had a one-man advantage, and the other team pulled the goalie with one minute of play left. One player got a breakaway and was heading toward the open goal with no one to check him.

Phillip reached the end of his patience level. The game was nearly over, and Neil hadn't made any attempt to join them or even add to the conversation.

The commentator's voice blared. "He shoots!" The television audience went wild.

Phillip reached into the box for the last ornament, purposely backing up so he completely blocked the screen as he bent over.

Neil jumped to his feet. "That does it!" he yelled. "What

do you think you're doing? The whole game you've been doing this!"

"He scores!" the commentator's voice shouted over the top of the crowd.

Phillip turned around, speaking to Neil through gritted teeth. "I can't believe you've been watching that stupid game the whole time Grace has been here. You should be putting up the tree with us, not sitting there with your face glued to the television."

"We could have done the tree after the game."

"It's taken us over an hour. Did you ever think that Grace would like to get home and get to bed at a decent hour since it's church tomorrow morning?"

"Then you could have done it just like you did, without being such a pain when I was watching the game."

"She doesn't come here all the time to watch you watch the television. She comes here to be with you, and most of the time you don't give her the time of day."

"If she's here to see me, it's strange that she seems to spend so much time with you."

"Maybe she wouldn't if she could spend the time with you. But I'm tired of playing second fiddle, Neil."

Except for the drone of the television, a charged silence hung in the air while Phillip waited for Neil's response.

Chapter 15

Grace couldn't believe her eyes or her ears. Not only were Phil and Neil fighting, they were fighting over her. She didn't know what to do.

"Maybe I should go home..." she barely managed to squeak out, although she didn't know how, without her car.

Phil dragged one hand over his face. "I'm sorry. I don't know what came over me. I was completely out of line. I apologize."

Neil sighed, then turned to Grace. "I'm sorry, too, Grace. Phil is right. I have been ignoring you. How can I make it up to you?"

Grace stared at the two men, her mind reeling too much to speak. First, Phil's words that he was tired of playing second fiddle echoed in her head. She hadn't realized he felt like that, but maybe she should have. Twice now she thought he had wanted to kiss her, and now she realized that she had read him correctly the first time, before she talked herself out of it. However, the reason she talked herself out of it so easily was because she had wanted to kiss him, too, and that was wrong.

And Neil. She'd convinced herself that their relationship was the same as it had been since they first started dating—they were both comfortable with not putting demands on each other's time. After spending so much time with Phil, every time she saw him, she wanted to see him more. The more she saw of Phil, the more she realized that her relationship with Neil wasn't merely comfortable. It was stagnant.

Nothing was happening the way she had it planned, and she didn't know what to do. Therefore, she would do nothing.

"It's okay," she mumbled. "I have an idea. Let's pick this up where we left off, and this time, we'll do it right. There are a few bare spots on the tree to fill up, and then we can finish off by putting Dale on her new home, the place she was meant to be."

The relief of the two men that they could carry on and all was normal again was almost tangible.

Rather sheepishly, Neil turned off the television and hung the last of the ornaments on the tree while Phil left the room, then returned with another box.

"Where did you go?" she asked as he set the large box on the coffee table.

"I did like you said and put Dale in a box to keep him safe. It worked, didn't it?"

As he spoke, Phil pulled the flaps open and started digging inside for Dale. What she saw made Grace's heart sink and her stomach tied in knots. "What is that?"

"It's newspaper. I used it to wrap Dale up. Pretty smart, huh?"

"You wrapped up a white crocheted angel in newspaper? Oh, Phil… What have you done?"

Sure enough, when Phil pulled Dale out, she was smudged with gray, especially on the outstretched wings.

Phil blinked, stared, and rubbed at the dark spots with one finger. "I don't understand. When Granny moved, she wrapped everything up in newspaper to keep it safe, so I thought I'd do the same with Dale."

Grace buried her face in her hands and shook her head. "Yes, your granny would have wrapped up her dishes, but they're made of glass. She would have washed them before she put them away. You're supposed to wrap ornaments and things that can't be washed in towels or white tissue paper."

Phil smiled weakly. "I guess we know that Dale can be washed...." His voice trailed off.

Grace sighed. Fortunately she'd bought another bag of cornstarch because she wanted to make Chinese Lemon Chicken this week. "We should probably do it tonight. You said you have family coming over on Monday evening?"

"Yes. And if they don't see that angel on top of the tree on Monday, I'm going to have to come up with some quick explanations. Especially if they bring Granny, which they might."

Neil turned to the door, then back to Grace. "I guess that answers the question of who drives you home tonight."

"Yes. We'd better go now."

Neil walked with Grace to the door, while Phil went into the bathroom to wash his hands after digging through the crumpled newspaper. As soon as the bathroom door closed, Neil spoke.

"I know we have to talk about this, but what happened tonight kind of tells me that this isn't working. I'm going to have to think things through, and then we'll get together and talk. I mean *really* get together and *really* talk."

Her heart sank, but Grace did agree. "Yes, I think you're right."

The bathroom door opened, ending their conversation. For the first time since she could remember, Neil gave her a gentle kiss on the lips instead of her cheek. But, it didn't feel like the kiss of a lover. It felt like a gentle way of saying goodbye.

Phil didn't have much to say during the drive to her apartment, nor did he say much as they washed Dale and cooked up another batch of the starch mixture. This time, Phil didn't master any artwork in the snow on the balcony; he simply did what he had to do to cool the mixture as quickly as possible.

Conversation wasn't as stilted as it could have been, but at the same time, nothing with any meaning passed between them the whole time they positioned Dale with the wire mesh and balloons, then propped her up with the books and chopsticks above the heat vent.

On his way out, Phil was through the door when he stopped, turned around, stepped back inside, and closed the door behind him.

"Do you love him?"

"I…" Grace let her voice trail off. She wanted to bide some time and ask him what he meant, but she knew perfectly well.

She'd never thought of Neil in the context of love. She'd thought about Neil in the context of safe.

Unlike her father and brother-in-law, Neil demanded nothing in his relationship with her. However, in retrospect, that also meant he gave what he expected, which wasn't much. Grace's predominant fear in any relationship was having to live under the same strict regime her family had to live under in order to please her father. Neil never expected her to live by a schedule because he wouldn't follow one himself. Grace hadn't thought of this as a bad thing until she discovered that the extension of that trait was that Neil was usually late for any planned activity. At first it bothered her, but Grace later learned to live with it, as no one was ever hurt by it. This was simply Neil asserting his autonomy.

Grace thought that was what she wanted out of a relationship, things her mother and sister never had—the freedom to go her own way and make her own decisions and do her own things. She had those things with Neil.

Neil was constant. His faith was solid, he never changed, he never did anything unpredictable. She knew what to expect with Neil. Yet, she could date Neil with no restrictions, and likewise, she placed no restrictions on him, with the mutual exclusions of fidelity and chastity.

Neil was everything she ever wanted in a man. Or was he?

Phil stepped closer, until they stood toe-to-toe. "Well?"

"I—I don't know," she stammered.

Phil's voice dropped to a low rumble. "Then know this."

Before she realized what he was going to do, Phil wrapped his arms around her and his mouth was on hers. He kissed her like she'd never been kissed before. With power and strength and confidence, and like he meant everything a kiss implied when holding her so close to his heart.

Fool that she was, she kissed him right back.

As quickly as the kiss began, it was over.

"Good night, Grace," Phil mumbled. He opened the door and left.

Too numb to do anything other than what she'd done a thousand times out of habit, Grace stepped into the hall to watch him go.

Phil didn't stop to wait for the elevator. He strode to the door for the stairwell, opened it, and he was gone.

"What do you mean, Phil isn't home? Where did he go?" Neil accepted the re-restarched angel from her and shrugged his shoulders. "I don't know. Now that you mention it, it is unusual for him to be gone on Sunday night. If he still isn't home by the time I go to bed, I'll put the angel on the tree for him and leave him a note that you were here."

Grace stood in the doorway, waiting for Neil to invite her in. He didn't.

"This is it, isn't it, Neil?"

"Yes. I've been doing a lot of thinking, and I'm sure you have, too. We can always be friends."

We can be friends. The death knell to any relationship. Except she knew that she really could always be friends with Neil. They didn't have the type of relationship that could break anyone's heart once it was over. She knew that now. What she had with Neil, she would always have. Nothing had been different this morning at church. Neil and Phil had picked her up, they'd sat together, gone out for lunch together, had fun together, just like they had in weeks gone by.

Grace didn't speak, so Neil continued. "Besides, I think we all know where your heart is, and I can't blame you. I guess I'll see you tomorrow night when you come to give Phil his guitar lesson. Good night, Grace."

"Okay. Good night, Neil."

The door closed.

This time she didn't wonder why he didn't kiss her as she left, nor did she wonder why he so seldom kissed her before. It simply wasn't there to begin with. Therefore, in his own way of saying it, Neil was right. Nothing between them had changed. They had been friends and nothing more, despite her delusions. The only change to their relationship was the title.

But, last night had changed whatever existed between her and Phil, and it scared her. Whether it was something on the top shelf at the grocery store, an obstacle to be overcome at work, or a challenging ministry situation at church, Phillip McLean always got what he wanted. When he set his mind on something, he worked—and he worked hard—until he got it. Whatever stood in his way didn't stand a chance.

Grace wouldn't be a conquest to be won. She refused to fall into the pattern of her mother and her sister and allow a man to take over her life and crush all her hopes and dreams. Then, when that was gone, she wouldn't live in fear of doing something wrong when there should have been nothing to be afraid of.

She didn't know that Phil would or could be that way, but she didn't want to take the chance. Up until now, she didn't have to worry about Phil. They'd had Neil between them, acting as a barrier, saving her from risk and potential disaster. Now, that was gone.

Grace walked to the car and drove home. Just because she was no longer officially with Neil didn't mean she had to stop seeing Phil or that she couldn't enjoy Phil's company. However, it did mean that she would have to be very careful and see what happened as time went on.

"No, that's not it. See how I've got my third finger? This is a C chord."

Phil repositioned his finger and strummed the chord. "Like this?"

"Yes. Now play the whole song, and I'll watch you."

Grace watched Phil pick through the new song, thoroughly impressed with his progress.

She also was very impressed by how things had gone since she'd officially broken up with Neil. Over a week had passed and nothing had changed between her and Phil. At least nothing had changed on Phil's side. After he'd kissed her, he had done nothing more, and he'd behaved the same way he always had. They talked the same way they always had. They prayed together the same way they always had. Whatever the reason for his impulsive action, he'd obviously worked it out of his system, and life went on as before.

It was she who had changed. At first she thought she would see Phil less because Neil was no longer a consideration. Instead, she found herself wanting to see Phil more, which wasn't possible, because she already saw him every day.

The coming of Christmas in a few days almost made her sad, because it meant that, on Christmas Day, she couldn't be with him. Instead of sitting with her during the service, he would be sitting with his family. Then, after the service, they would all be going together to his parents' house for the day. Likewise, as soon as the service ended, Grace would begin the long drive to her own parents' house, which she wasn't exactly looking forward to. The only bonus was that she could announce that she was officially single again, and her sister would have to stop bothering her about when she was going to marry Neil.

Phil strummed the last chord of the song, then shook the guitar for added effect.

Grace smiled. "Very funny, but that was still pretty good. I would think your fingers have had enough and it's time to pack up."

Phil shook his hand in the air. "Yeah, but it's not nearly as bad as when I first started."

"Come on, let's get your amp and guitar out of here. It was crowded in your living room before, but now with the Christmas tree set up, there's barely room to walk."

Grace stood at the same time as Phil. She reached for his tuning meter at the same time as he stepped around the coffee table to turn off the amp.

Grace turned to go to the kitchen, but when she took her first step, she could feel the patch cord between the guitar and the amp under her toes moving as Phil picked up his guitar. As quickly as she could move so she didn't cause him to ruin the plug, Grace hopped up, but in so doing, her toes caught the leg of the coffee table.

"Ouch!" she yelped and hopped up on the other foot. The sudden movement caused her to back up, but she'd forgotten about the amp, which caught her in the back of her knee.

Grace felt herself starting to topple. She flailed her arms in an attempt to regain her balance, but she couldn't stop herself from going down.

"Grace!" Phil called out. He reached over the coffee table to grab her by the arm, but he missed.

Grace fell backward, right into the Christmas tree. Before she crumpled to the ground, a strong hand slipped around her waist, holding her up. Behind her, the tree bounced with a crash against the living-room window, then fell to the floor. All around her echoed the tinkling of breaking glass and clunking of metallic ornaments hitting each other before everything came to a rest at various places around the tree, which lay at her feet.

Strong arms wrapped around her, holding her tight, even though she'd long since regained her balance.

"Are you okay?" Phil murmured in her ear.

She was standing, but she didn't know if she was okay. With Phil's arms around her, some silly misfiring neuron in her brain wanted him to kiss her.

Grace lifted her hands and pushed her palms against his chest, forcing him to release her. "I'm fine. I'm so sorry about your tree. Let me pick everything up."

"We can all do it together. Neil? Can you go get a bag or something?"

In a few seconds, Neil returned with a plastic grocery bag, and they all started picking up the glass pieces from the broken balls. When enough was cleared that they could get close, Phil and Neil righted the tree and pushed it back into place.

With the tree once more standing straight, Phil reached down and picked up Dale. He brushed off a few broken pieces and shook the angel out. "Poor Dale," he mumbled. "That must have been quite a fall. Fortunately, there's nothing on him that is breakable."

Grace nodded. "Good thing. Tomorrow is Christmas Eve, and you're taking Dale to your parents' house Christmas morning, right?"

"Yup."

Phil reached up and returned Dale to her place atop the bedraggled tree. "There. Everything looks better already."

Grace looked up at Dale as she began to straighten the popcorn garland. "It shouldn't take long to… Oh, no. What's that!?" She inched closer and stood on her tiptoes to see Dale better. "Blood! Phil! You're bleeding!"

Phil raised his hands, fanned his fingers out, then stuck one finger in his mouth. "It's nothing," he muttered around his finger. "I must have cut myself with a piece of broken glass from those ornaments."

"Never mind your finger. Look at Dale."

All noise in the room faded into a timeless void as all three of them looked up at Dale. A small spot of bright red blood showed vividly on the left wing.

The three of them groaned in unison.

"Well," Grace mumbled, "I guess we're going back to my house, aren't we, Phil?"

Chapter 16

"Merry Christmas, Neil!"

"Merry Christmas, Phil!"

Phil and Neil patted each other on the shoulders, then went their separate ways to get ready for church. Since Neil had the shower first, Phillip went into the living room and plugged in the lights for the Christmas tree while he waited for his turn.

Almost reverently, he looked up at the tree and smiled as Dale looked back down at him. At least Phillip *thought* Dale was looking down.

It was almost like he'd come to know the little angel on a personal basis, he'd done so much with him.

With the utmost care, Phillip plucked Dale from the top branch and brought him down.

It had seemed like so long ago that he'd first brought Dale home. That day had been the start of the best time of his life, and the worst—the start of when he got to know Grace.

He turned Dale over in his hand, studying the perfect stitches and the perfect uniformity of the shaping, which wouldn't have been possible without Grace.

Grace. He didn't know exactly when he'd fallen in love with her, but the time since he'd been able to admit it to himself had been the most frustrating of his life.

He wanted to marry Grace, but he didn't think she wanted to marry him. When he made his decision, he'd promised God that he would wait until the right time to propose, but that time had not come. Instead, he'd used almost all of his inner strength to do nothing except build their friendship as slowly as he could, if seeing her every day could be called slow, especially after Neil told him the other Sunday that he was no longer officially seeing Grace.

Phil had never prayed so much or so long in his life, but that was never a bad thing. He wanted God's grace and blessing on his marriage, and he therefore would follow God's guidelines.

He'd talked to Grace about marriage in general a few times without actually proposing, and it was a good thing he hadn't. During those times he'd learned that she had some kind of problem with the structure of her family, something to do with her father. Because of that, Grace was too frightened to take that big step into marriage, which was why she had connected with Neil. Neil didn't want to get married either. In that regard, the two of them would have been a perfect match.

Except, Phillip knew Neil wasn't the match for Grace. He was. But, above all, Phillip wanted Grace to be happy, even if that meant a sacrifice for him. He loved her so much that he knew he would never be able to marry anyone else.

Again, he studied Dale. The angel truly had become more than a Christmas ornament. Dale really had become his guardian angel. It was because of Dale that he'd come to know Grace. For that reason alone, Phillip had become quite fond of the little angel, and he knew that Grace had become quite fond of Dale, too.

Suddenly, Phillip's throat went dry, and his heart began to pound.

Dale had been the catalyst that allowed them to get to know each other, and Dale could also be the catalyst to see them married.

As soon as Neil took one step out of the bathroom, Phillip was in. He showered, shaved, dressed, and was out the door in record time.

Also in record time, he was at the door of Grace's apartment building.

He pushed the button, shuffling his feet until she answered.

"Hi, Grace. Merry Christmas."

"Phil? What are you doing here? Oh, and Merry Christmas to you, too."

"I've got Dale. I have to see you."

"Dale? Oh, no. Not today. What happened this time? Or do I not want to know?"

The buzzer sounded before she finished speaking. Phillip yanked the door open and ran to the elevator.

When the elevator door opened at Grace's floor, she was already there, right at the elevator door.

She grabbed Dale out of his hands. "We've got half an hour before we have to leave for church." She turned Dale over a few times. "What's wrong? I don't see anything."

Phil stepped out of the elevator and let the door close so it could go to the next person who pushed the button on another floor. He let one hand rest on Grace's shoulder, and with the other, he pointed to the center of Dale's chest.

"Right here. It's his heart. It's broken."

"I don't understand."

"Don't you see? It's Dale that drew us together, and even though he didn't have to, he's kept on pulling us together.

When Christmas is over, he's going to be packed up in a box for another year, and his job isn't done. He's been trying to tell us something, and we haven't been listening. He's been telling us that we should be more than friends."

"That's ridiculous. It's just a creation made by man, or rather woman. Your granny."

"Maybe so, but still, the point is made. I love you, Grace, and I guess what I'm doing is asking if you'll marry me."

"Marry you? I...I don't know."

Phillip couldn't stop his hand from trembling as he reached down and rested his fingertips on Grace's cheek. It almost hurt to ask, but he had to know for sure. "Do you love me?"

He could see the interplay of her thoughts in her big brown eyes. Her eyes flickered slightly as she focused on his right eye, then his left, then fixed her gaze on his right eye as she continued to think.

If she said she didn't know, like when he asked if she loved Neil, he knew that all would be lost.

His heart pounded so hard in his chest it almost hurt.

"Yes."

Phillip felt himself break out into a slow, lazy grin. "Then there shouldn't be a question. You know I'd never do anything to hurt you. If you're still nervous or if I did anything wrong, I'd go for counseling or whatever you wanted me to do. I know you said you wished your mother and father would go."

"You'd do that for me?"

He would have done anything for her. By saying it out loud, he was confirming both to her and to himself how much he loved her. "Yes, I would do that for you. In fact, how about if we start with premarital counseling?"

Grace's eyes glassed over, and Phillip cringed inside, thinking she was going to cry, but she blinked rapidly a few times, then swallowed hard.

"I think that would be a great start. I guess that means that I would like to marry you."

No words would come. Instead, Phillip removed Dale from her shaking hands, and with Dale hanging from his fingertips, he wrapped his arms around Grace and kissed her with all the love in his heart.

The ding of the elevator door behind him caused them to separate. With Dale in one hand and Grace's hand in his other, Phillip walked slowly down the hall with Grace, back to her apartment.

"I think it's time to get your coat on and go to church. I can hardly wait to tell everyone that it's official, that we're engaged. I guess that also means we have to make up our minds on what we're going to do today. Do you want to go to my parents' place for Christmas Day or yours?"

"I'd love to tell my sister I'm finally getting married, but I think I'd rather go to your parents' house with your family. After everything that's happened, I really want to see Dale on top of your parents' tree."

While Grace slipped on her boots, Phillip held up his Christmas angel and smiled. Now, not only did the angel signify the celebration of his Savior's birth, it also signified the start of his new life together with Grace.

"I'm ready. Let's go."

Phillip couldn't stop himself. Before they went out in public together, he had to kiss her one more time.

When he finally released her, he kept his head bowed, their foreheads touching, and gave her one more small kiss.

"Merry Christmas, Grace."

She smiled back. "Yes. It is a Merry Christmas."

* * * * *

REQUEST YOUR FREE BOOKS!

2 FREE INSPIRATIONAL NOVELS
PLUS 2
FREE
MYSTERY GIFTS

Love Inspired

YES! Please send me 2 FREE Love Inspired® novels and my 2 FREE mystery gifts (gifts are worth about $10). After receiving them, if I don't wish to receive any more books, I can return the shipping statement marked "cancel." If I don't cancel, I will receive 6 brand-new novels every month and be billed just $4.74 per book in the U.S. or $5.24 per book in Canada. That's a savings of at least 21% off the cover price. It's quite a bargain! Shipping and handling is just 50¢ per book in the U.S. and 75¢ per book in Canada.* I understand that accepting the 2 free books and gifts places me under no obligation to buy anything. I can always return a shipment and cancel at any time. Even if I never buy another book, the two free books and gifts are mine to keep forever.

105/305 IDN F49N

Name	(PLEASE PRINT)

Address	Apt. #

City	State/Prov.	Zip/Postal Code

Signature (if under 18, a parent or guardian must sign)

Mail to the Harlequin® Reader Service:
IN U.S.A.: P.O. Box 1867, Buffalo, NY 14240-1867
IN CANADA: P.O. Box 609, Fort Erie, Ontario L2A 5X3

**Are you a subscriber to Love Inspired books
and want to receive the larger-print edition?
Call 1-800-873-8635 or visit www.ReaderService.com.**

* Terms and prices subject to change without notice. Prices do not include applicable taxes. Sales tax applicable in N.Y. Canadian residents will be charged applicable taxes. Offer not valid in Quebec. This offer is limited to one order per household. Not valid for current subscribers to Love Inspired books. All orders subject to credit approval. Credit or debit balances in a customer's account(s) may be offset by any other outstanding balance owed by or to the customer. Please allow 4 to 6 weeks for delivery. Offer available while quantities last.

Your Privacy—The Harlequin® Reader Service is committed to protecting your privacy. Our Privacy Policy is available online at www.ReaderService.com or upon request from the Harlequin Reader Service.
We make a portion of our mailing list available to reputable third parties that offer products we believe may interest you. If you prefer that we not exchange your name with third parties, or if you wish to clarify or modify your communication preferences, please visit us at www.ReaderService.com/consumerchoice or write to us at Harlequin Reader Service Preference Service, P.O. Box 9062, Buffalo, NY 14269. Include your complete name and address.

LIDIR13R

REQUEST YOUR FREE BOOKS!

2 FREE INSPIRATIONAL NOVELS
PLUS 2
FREE
MYSTERY GIFTS

Love Inspired.
HISTORICAL
INSPIRATIONAL HISTORICAL ROMANCE

YES! Please send me 2 FREE Love Inspired® Historical novels and my 2 FREE mystery gifts (gifts are worth about $10). After receiving them, if I don't wish to receive any more books, I can return the shipping statement marked "cancel." If I don't cancel, I will receive 4 brand-new novels every month and be billed just $4.74 per book in the U.S. or $5.24 per book in Canada. That's a savings of at least 21% off the cover price. It's quite a bargain! Shipping and handling is just 50¢ per book in the U.S. and 75¢ per book in Canada.* I understand that accepting the 2 free books and gifts places me under no obligation to buy anything. I can always return a shipment and cancel at any time. Even if I never buy another book, the two free books and gifts are mine to keep forever.

102/302 IDN F5CY

Name _____ (PLEASE PRINT) _____

Address _____ Apt. # _____

City _____ State/Prov. _____ Zip/Postal Code _____

Signature (if under 18, a parent or guardian must sign)

Mail to the **Harlequin® Reader Service:**
IN U.S.A.: P.O. Box 1867, Buffalo, NY 14240-1867
IN CANADA: P.O. Box 609, Fort Erie, Ontario L2A 5X3

Want to try two free books from another series?
Call 1-800-873-8635 or visit www.ReaderService.com.

* Terms and prices subject to change without notice. Prices do not include applicable taxes. Sales tax applicable in N.Y. Canadian residents will be charged applicable taxes. Offer not valid in Quebec. This offer is limited to one order per household. Not valid for current subscribers to Love Inspired Historical books. All orders subject to credit approval. Credit or debit balances in a customer's account(s) may be offset by any other outstanding balance owed by or to the customer. Please allow 4 to 6 weeks for delivery. Offer available while quantities last.

Your Privacy—The Harlequin® Reader Service is committed to protecting your privacy. Our Privacy Policy is available online at www.ReaderService.com or upon request from the Harlequin Reader Service.

We make a portion of our mailing list available to reputable third parties that offer products we believe may interest you. If you prefer that we not exchange your name with third parties, or if you wish to clarify or modify your communication preferences, please visit us at www.ReaderService.com/consumerschoice or write to us at Harlequin Reader Service Preference Service, P.O. Box 9062, Buffalo, NY 14269. Include your complete name and address.

LIHDIR13R

ReaderService.com

Manage your account online!

- Review your order history
- Manage your payments
- Update your address

*We've designed
the Harlequin® Reader Service
website just for you.*

Enjoy all the features!

- Reader excerpts from any series
- Respond to mailings and
  special monthly offers
- Discover new series available to you
- Browse the Bonus Bucks catalog
- Share your feedback

Visit us at:
ReaderService.com